— A *Felicity* MYSTERY —

# PERIL AT KING'S CREEK

by Elizabeth McDavid Jones

Questions or comments? Call 1-800-845-0005,
visit **americangirl.com**, or write to Customer Service,
American Girl, 8400 Fairway Place, Middleton, WI 53562-0497.

Printed in China
12 13 14 15 16 17 LEO 16 15 14 13 12 11

All American Girl marks, American Girl Mysteries®, Felicity®, and
Felicity Merriman® are trademarks of American Girl.

This book is a work of fiction. Any similarity to real persons, living or dead,
is coincidental and not intended by American Girl. References to real events,
people, or places are used fictitiously. Other names, characters, places, and
incidents are the products of imagination.

PICTURE CREDITS
The following individuals and organizations have generously
given permission to reprint illustrations contained in "Looking Back":
pp. 158–159—plantation home, Bruce Roberts; battle scene, North Wind
Picture Archives; pp. 160–161—British raid, North Wind Picture Archives;
Governor Dunmore, The Library of Virginia; mounted soldier,
North Wind Picture Archives; pp. 162–163—quill and inkpot,
© Royalty Free/Corbis; Declaration of Independence, © Joseph Sohm/Corbis;
Catherine Schuyler scene, The Granger Collection, New York; pp. 164–165—
Sybil Ludington statue, Putnam County Historion;
signing of Declaration of Independence, North Wind Picture Archives;
battle scene, North Wind Picture Archives.

Illustrations by Jean-Paul Tibbles

Library of Congress Cataloging-in-Publication Data

Jones, Elizabeth McDavid, 1958–
Peril at King's Creek : a Felicity mystery  /  by Elizabeth McDavid Jones ;
        p.  cm. — "American Girl." "American girl mysteries."
Summary: In 1776, eleven-year-old Felicity suspects that an amateur naturalist
visiting her family's Virginia plantation may actually be a British spy
mapping Patriot plantations in advance of British raids. Includes historical
information about the Revolutionary War.
ISBN 978-1-59369-102-8 — ISBN 978-1-59369-101-1 (pbk.)
1. Virginia—History—Revolution, 1775–1783— Juvenile fiction.
2. United States—History—Revolution, 1775–1783— Juvenile fiction.
[1. Virginia—History—Revolution, 1775–1783—Fiction. 2. United States—
History—Revolution, 1775–1783—Fiction.
3. Spies—Fiction. 4. Plantation life—Virginia—Fiction.] I. Title.
PZ7.J6855Pe 2006            [Fic]—dc22            2006042910

*To Tristan William Jones,*
*who joined our family during the*
*writing of this book and made us all*
*wonder how we'd ever lived without him*

# TABLE OF CONTENTS

# 1
## AN INTERESTING GUEST

Felicity Merriman headed up the white shell path that led to the stable at King's Creek Plantation, the plantation that had been her grandfather's and now belonged to Felicity's family. She walked as briskly as she could, wishing her stays weren't laced quite so tightly. If they weren't, she would run! Sweat trickled down her face, and her shift clung damply to her skin. How hot it was for so early in June!

The plantation, on a bluff above the York River, was usually cooled by the river's gentle breezes. Today, though, not a breath of air stirred the willows on the riverbank or the leaves of the tall tulip poplar trees on the plantation's grounds. Felicity was sure

1

it was the hottest day yet since her family had arrived here to spend the summer.

This late in the morning, Lester, the head groom, would already have turned Penny and Patriot out into the paddock behind the stable with the other mares and foals. Penny was Felicity's copper-colored mare, and Patriot was Penny's foal.

When Felicity reached the paddock, she hiked up her skirt and clambered up to sit on the top rail of the fence, hooking her feet on the rail below. The mares were grazing peacefully, most of them facing the same way, their noses downwind. Penny's chestnut coat glinted in the bright sunlight like the copper penny for which she was named. Felicity sighed happily. Was there another horse any-where in the colony of Virginia so fine and swift as Penny?

Sometimes Felicity still marveled that Penny was really hers. She had helped Penny escape from her previous owner, Jiggy Nye, who had been cruel to Penny, and she hadn't known then whether or not she would ever see Penny again. Later, Penny had come to be owned by Grandfather's neighbor Mr. Wentworth, and Grandfather had bought her for Felicity.

A heaviness came into Felicity's heart when she thought of Grandfather. He had died last winter, and she missed him terribly. She had found, though, that if she turned her thoughts to the good times she and Grandfather had shared, the heaviness would lift, so she did that, remembering how Grandfather had been the one to tell her Penny was going to be a mother. And now, here was Patriot, dashing around the pasture with the other foals.

Felicity smiled. The foals looked as if they were playing tag. They were nipping each other and tearing off to one end of the pasture, then back again. Patriot, with his shiny black coat, was the youngest foal, yet he was faster than all the others.

"Ah, little Patriot," Felicity breathed with pride. "You're smaller than the other foals, but you have twice the spirit. I named you well. You are like the Patriot army. And you, like the army, will be the strongest in the end. Just wait and see."

Patriot, as if he had heard, took off running, kicking his heels in the air with little bucking jumps. Felicity laughed. Then she put two fingers to her lips and whistled sharply, the way Ben, her father's apprentice, had taught her. Penny always came on the run at Felicity's whistle. She knew Felicity would have a treat for her—a big fat carrot, a juicy apple, or a lump or two of sugar.

Penny's ears flicked, her head came up, and she gave a whicker—calling Patriot, Felicity supposed. Penny trotted over to the fence, with Patriot at her heels. Felicity held the sugar lumps she had saved from her breakfast in her closed fist while Penny's big nostrils sniffed her hand, and the long whiskery hairs on her nose trembled. Then Felicity opened her hand and Penny's soft lips had the sugar, and she was crunching it. Felicity rubbed

4

Penny's muzzle and her soft nose.

After Penny had had her treat, Felicity slipped the rope loop of the lead shank she had brought with her over Penny's head. Then Felicity led her to the stable, with Patriot following, and saddled her. Patriot nickered when he was left alone in the stall. "My little Patriot," Felicity said gently. "You wait here for your mama. Nan and I will come back later and play with you, I promise." Felicity's little sister Nan was learning to ride this summer, and she had been helping Felicity take care of Penny and Patriot. Nan was fond of both horses, but especially of Patriot. She had always adored baby animals.

Felicity gave Patriot one more reassuring pat, then led Penny out of the stable and mounted her. Soon Felicity and Penny were off, cantering through the upper pasture, Felicity's straw hat bobbing by its ribbon on the back of her neck. The wind rushed past Felicity's hot cheeks, and the ground sped away beneath her. Filled with exhilaration, she leaned low and urged Penny on, up and over the pasture fence.

As they cantered along the path that ran along the edge of the woods, Felicity's conscience pricked her. She knew she shouldn't be taking Penny on such a long ride; she had promised Mother that she would be back by one o'clock for dinner.

Their neighbors the Wentworths were coming to dine with them, and Felicity dreaded it. Mother expected Felicity, since she was eleven, to join the adults when there was company and listen politely to adult conversation. But it was so hard to do when the company was someone like Mrs. Wentworth. Mrs. Wentworth dearly loved to talk, and she didn't much like to listen, though she expected everyone to listen to her.

Thinking about having to suffer through a dinner with Mrs. Wentworth made Felicity feel hot all over again. So she ignored her guilty conscience, bent over Penny, and let herself feel Penny's stride. It seemed that she and Penny were one, sailing along on the wind with the trees whizzing by. Time seemed to stop and nothing existed but the two of them.

When Felicity and Penny finally headed back to the stable, Felicity realized that she had been gone much longer than she'd meant to be. The Wentworths' carriage was parked outside the stable, and Lester had already unhitched the matched team of dappled gray horses and put them into stalls. "Oh, dear," Felicity said. "I hope I'm not late for dinner." She quickly unsaddled Penny, rubbed her down, and hurried to the house.

Inside, Felicity slipped up the servants' stairway to her bedchamber, splashed water from the china basin onto her face and neck, and smoothed her hair. Downstairs she could hear the planter's clock in the entrance hall chiming one o'clock. She had made it! But there was no time to change her gown.

Felicity rushed from her room and down the staircase, thinking enviously of Nan and her brother William and even baby Polly, who were all too young for company dinners. They got to eat in the kitchen house, in back of the big house, with the cook Lucy and her children. Felicity sighed. Sometimes it was hard to be the oldest. She couldn't wait until Nan, who was nearly eight, would be old enough to join her in the dining room when the Wentworths came to call.

Felicity hurried into the dining room, going so fast that she nearly slipped on the polished floor of the entrance hall. The serving maids had already brought in food from the kitchen and set it on the sideboard. There was ham and mutton, a steaming plate of buckwheat cakes, candied apples, and huckleberries in thick cream. Tildy, in her white turban and crisp white apron, stood by to serve.

In the gilt mirror above the sideboard, the long cherrywood dining table was reflected, and Felicity could see Mother and the dinner guests already seated. Father was not at the table because he had stayed in Williamsburg for the summer to run his store. Felicity was eagerly looking forward to his visit in a few weeks. Mother sat at the head of the table, with Mr. and Mrs. Wentworth on either side of her. Beside Mr. Wentworth sat a young man wearing a fancy coat with gold buttons and ruffles at the wrists. His thick black hair was pulled back in a queue.

Felicity remembered that Mother had told her the Wentworths would be bringing their houseguest, someone from Philadelphia. The man in the fancy coat must be the Wentworths' visitor—which meant that the proper seating for Felicity would be beside Mrs. Wentworth.

Felicity moved to stand behind that chair and waited to be introduced. Mother nodded to her. "There you are, Daughter," Mother said. "Mr. Haskall, this is my eldest daughter, Felicity."

Mr. Haskall and Mr. Wentworth had politely stood up when Felicity came into the room. Felicity curtsied. "Pleased to make your acquaintance, Mr. Haskall," she said.

"And yours, Miss Merriman," Mr. Haskall answered with a bow.

Felicity thought he looked vaguely familiar. She sat down, trying to place him, and at first she didn't notice Mrs. Wentworth leaning toward her—until Mrs. Wentworth sniffed, very loudly. "Do I smell . . . horse?" Mrs. Wentworth asked, turning up her nose.

Felicity felt herself flush, and her hands flew up to cover her face. Mr. Wentworth cleared his throat. Mother frowned. Mr. Haskall wrinkled his forehead, sniffed, and said, "Horse? My dear Mrs. Wentworth, I don't smell a thing."

"Don't you?" said Mrs. Wentworth, pulling back from Felicity. "Perhaps it is the mutton."

Mother raised an eyebrow.

"Mrs. Merriman," stammered Mrs. Wentworth. "I didn't mean to imply that the mutton . . ." She stopped, her face as red as the pickled beets in Mother's crystal dish. Then she cleared her throat, spread out her napkin, and said brightly, "Well. Everything looks so delicious. And I am quite famished. Are you not famished, Mr. Haskall?"

"Oh, quite famished indeed," Mr. Haskall said. He cast a quick, amused glance in Felicity's direction, his brown eyes twinkling. As he did so, Felicity's heart gave a little jump. She had seen Mr. Haskall before. She was sure of it.

But where?

# 2
## DISTURBING NEWS

"Shall we begin, then?" said Mother.

Tildy brought the platters and bowls of food from the sideboard and handed them to Mother, who passed them to the guests. Soon silverware clinked on china as everyone began to eat.

While the adults chatted, Felicity tried to recall where she had seen Mr. Haskall before. Perhaps she'd met him on another occasion when the Wentworths had come to dine, though she didn't think so. Had she met him in Williamsburg? She would have liked to ask him, but it wasn't proper for children to speak unless an adult spoke to them first.

Felicity ate slowly, listening to the conversation. Usually when Mrs. Wentworth talked, Felicity's mind wandered, but today Mrs.

# DISTURBING NEWS

Wentworth was talking about Mr. Haskall—
more than she was letting Mr. Haskall talk,
to be sure—and Felicity, now curious about
the Wentworths' visitor, listened carefully.

The more she heard, the more puzzled
Felicity became. Mr. Haskall was from Philadelphia, Mrs. Wentworth said, and he was
traveling to Charles Town in South Carolina
to visit his sister. He and the Wentworths had
a mutual friend in Philadelphia, and it was
that friend who had proposed he stop at the
Wentworths' on his way.

"How are you liking our colony, Mr.
Haskall?" asked Mother as she passed the
sterling silver gravy boat.

"I'm charmed, actually," said Mr. Haskall.
He took the gravy boat from Mr. Wentworth
and poured steaming red-eye gravy over thick
slices of ham on his plate. "I've never been
farther south than Baltimore, and I'm finding
the area quite to my liking."

Felicity screwed her mouth to the side.
She must have been mistaken about having

seen Mr. Haskall before. If he had never been to Virginia, she couldn't possibly have met him. Perhaps it was only that he looked like someone else she had met.

"I'm particularly interested in your southern plantations," Mr. Haskall was going on. "They're so different from our farms in Pennsylvania. In fact, I was hoping I might impose on you, Mrs. Merriman, to show me around King's Creek Plantation."

"'Twould be no imposition at all," said Mother. "I'm certain Mr. Tate, our overseer, would be happy to accompany us on a tour of the grounds."

After dessert—a boiled plum pudding— Felicity walked with Mother and Mr. Haskall about the grounds of the plantation. The Wentworths, complaining of the afternoon heat, stayed in the parlor. The tour began in the front, on the river side, where Felicity, Mother, the overseer Mr. Tate, and Mr. Haskall strolled through the terraced gardens planted with flowers, shrubs, vegetables, and herbs.

Mr. Tate pointed out the fields above the river, where corn, wheat, and oats grew, and the pastures, where cattle and sheep grazed.

After they had viewed the formal garden at the side of the house, with its bricked walkways and sculpted shrubbery, Mr. Haskall asked to see the stable. "Mr. Wentworth spoke highly of your horses, Mrs. Merriman. Especially a certain chestnut mare..."

"Ah, that would be Penny," Mother said, smiling. "She belongs to Felicity, actually. I'm sure Felicity would be happy to show her to you."

The stable was made of brick and lined with arches, and it had rows of roomy stalls inside. Penny and Patriot were outside in the paddock behind the stable. Felicity's heart swelled with pride as she pointed them out to Mr. Haskall.

"Penny is the fastest horse here on the plantation," said Felicity. "That's why Father uses her for his commissary work for the Patriot Army—"

She stopped, unsure whether it had been wise to mention that Father was helping the Patriot cause. After all, the Wentworths were strong Loyalists; perhaps Mr. Haskall was also a Loyalist. She glanced at Mother to see whether Mother looked disapproving, but Mother was nodding. So Felicity told herself it was all right. After all, Father's work was not a secret. Everyone in Williamsburg knew what he was doing. Besides, she didn't think Mr. Haskall had even noticed what she had said. He was too busy admiring Penny.

"She's a fine horse indeed, Miss Merriman," he said. "Tall and graceful, with such a light, elegant neck. Her head so intelligent and alert. And long, strong legs and strong quarters. No doubt she runs like the wind."

"Oh, yes," said Felicity. "And she jumps as well as she runs."

"Her colt is a handsome one, too," said Mr. Haskall. "He looks as if he will be every bit as fast as his mother. You're a fortunate

young lady to own such splendid horses."
Felicity beamed.

Through the rest of the tour, Mr. Haskall
asked Mother and Mr. Tate questions about
the plantation, its workings, and its grounds.
He wanted to know how extensive the
plantation's holdings were, and Mother told
him that King's Creek land extended from
King's Creek to Philgate's Creek, where an
old footpath led through the woods to
Yorktown.

As they were walking back to the house
along the pasture fence at the edge of the
woods, Mr. Haskall suddenly exclaimed and
bent down to examine a plant with heart-
shaped leaves and purplish-brown flowers.
"By the king's realm! This is Virginia snakeroot, is it not, Mrs. Merriman? I was hoping
to find a specimen while I was here!"

Mother looked at the plant and shook her
head. "My father would've known," she said
with some sadness. "But he passed away last
winter."

Mr. Haskall expressed sympathy.

"Thank you," said Mother. "He knew a great deal about everything growing wild in these woods. What is your interest, Mr. Haskall?"

Mr. Haskall explained that he was an amateur naturalist—someone who studied plants and animals—and he was interested in collecting plant specimens not native to his own area. "Might I have permission to walk or ride sometimes on your grounds and in the surrounding woods to gather plant specimens?" he asked.

"Why, certainly," said Mrs. Merriman. "Feel free to do so at your will."

When they returned to the house, a neighboring plantation owner, Mr. Peabody, was waiting for Mother in the parlor with the Wentworths. The parlor was Felicity's favorite room in the house. Because it was so fancy, though, she was allowed to go in only when there was company. The furniture in the parlor was made of mahogany, and so was the floor, and when it was freshly polished, the whole room shone with a dark gleam like sun-ripened purple grapes. Mother always kept fresh flowers from the garden, whatever was in season, in a crystal bowl on the side table and in a vase on the mantel. Today, Felicity noted, the flowers were pale blue hydrangeas.

Mr. Peabody was sitting in a damask wing chair before the fireplace, chatting with the Wentworths, who sat on a sofa near his chair. The gentlemen stood up when Mother came into the parlor, and Mr. Peabody greeted her and Felicity and Mr. Haskall, with whom he was already acquainted.

"I haven't seen you lately around Rock Springs Farm, Mr. Haskall," said Mr. Peabody. Rock Springs Farm was the name of Mr. Peabody's plantation. "I trust, then, that you have finished collecting your plant specimens on my grounds?"

"Yes, as a matter of fact, I have," said Mr. Haskall, "and I am obliged to you for allowing me free rein on your grounds for my explorations."

"Did you find anything of interest?" asked Mr. Peabody, resting a hand inside his open waistcoat.

"Oh, quite," said Mr. Haskall agreeably. "There's nothing so fascinating to me as the natural world."

Mr. Peabody looked pleased and expectant—hoping, Felicity guessed, for Mr. Haskall to elaborate on his discoveries. Instead, Mr. Haskall added, "And I was honored that you allowed me to ride Midnight. What a marvelous animal!"

Felicity remembered the first time she'd seen Mr. Peabody's black mare, Midnight. Mr. Peabody had ridden her when he came to King's Creek to visit Grandfather, and Midnight had been turned out to pasture with the other mares. Midnight, a thoroughbred like Penny, loved to run, and Felicity had watched in awe as Penny and Midnight flashed neck and neck through the pasture, their shoulders stretched out and their tails streaming behind them like a coppery-black banner.

"Ah, Midnight," said Mother, smiling. "My father tried to buy Midnight from you, if I recall."

"Indeed, more than once," said Mr. Peabody. "He was quite put out because I wouldn't sell her. But I would never have parted with her. She was the prize of my stable, as your father well knew." Abruptly, he stopped speaking and massaged his brow as if it pained him. "But now it seems I have lost her anyway," Mr. Peabody continued. "She went missing yesterday, and I fear she's been stolen."

Felicity's stomach tightened. If someone had stolen Mr. Peabody's prize mare, then perhaps Penny was also at risk.

Mother put a hand to her bodice. "Oh, surely not," she said. "What makes you think so?"

"I can't account for her disappearance any

other way," said Mr. Peabody, the weathered wrinkles around his eyes deepening. "No fences were down, no gates left open, no other horses missing. She simply vanished from the paddock yesterday while I was away in Yorktown."

"Midnight is a spirited mare. Perhaps she jumped a fence and wandered away," suggested Mr. Haskall.

Mr. Peabody shook his head so vigorously that the curls of his wig jiggled. "I don't think Midnight would have gone far on her own— she loved her cozy barn and her morning oats too dearly. Yet we've found no trace of her. I'm afraid I can draw no other conclusion but that she was stolen. Needless to say, I'm sick about her loss."

Felicity sympathized with Mr. Peabody. How terrible she would feel if Penny went missing.

"A thief about!" exclaimed Mrs. Wentworth, jumping up from the sofa all in a dither. As she stood, her gown billowed up like a sail in the wind. "Mr. Wentworth, we must hurry home at once to see whether any of our own horses are missing!"

"Calm yourself, my dear," Mr. Wentworth said, patting his wife on the arm. Then, turning to Mr. Peabody, he inquired, "Peabody, my man, did you find any signs of an intruder?"

"None," said Mr. Peabody, frowning. "But the sheriff suggested that Patriot soldiers might have made off with Midnight. Seems there's been trouble with them in the area."

"Aye, those ragtag soldiers have no military discipline at all. They wander off at will, I hear—just leave their regiments and head on home whenever they please," Mr. Wentworth agreed. "If 'twas one of them, then both Midnight and the scoundrel who took her are probably long gone."

"I fear you're right," said Mr. Peabody with a heavy sigh. Then a shadow crossed his face. "But enough of that. I'm afraid I have come with even more disturbing news."

He hesitated, adjusting his cravat in a nervous gesture. "I don't wish to frighten you unnecessarily, Mrs. Merriman—you, a woman alone with four young children, and your husband away in Williamsburg— yet I think it important that you be aware of what is happening to the south of us."

Fear tickled at the edge of Felicity's mind. What was Mr. Peabody talking about?

"Please, tell us what you think we should know, Mr. Peabody," said Mother.

Mr. Peabody shifted his weight from one foot to the other, as if he wished he did not have to deliver the news at all. "As I mentioned, I was in Yorktown yesterday on business. The town was abuzz with reports that Governor Dunmore's troops had raided some plantations along the James River. In the dark of night, barns and stables were burned, and crops in the field—"

"I've been hearing such things for months," Mrs. Wentworth broke in huffily, "and they must be hateful rumors. Lord Dunmore would

never behave so abominably." She turned
to Mother. "Mrs. Merriman, didn't Lady
Dunmore invite Felicity to their palace a year
ago December?"

"Well, yes, she did, Mrs. Wentworth," said
Mother, "but—"

"There you have it," Mrs. Wentworth
asserted with a bob of her chin. "The reports
about Lord Dunmore are obviously false."

"As you know, Mrs. Wentworth, much
has changed since those carefree days," said
Mr. Peabody sadly.

Felicity nodded her agreement. Only a
year ago, Lord Dunmore had been the British
governor of Virginia. The winter before last,
Felicity had attended a dance lesson at his
residence, the lavish Governor's Palace in
Williamsburg. But since war had broken out
between the British king and the Patriots,
the governor had become more and more
hostile to his subjects. Relations between the
governor and the colonists had only gotten
worse, and last summer the governor had

fled Williamsburg. He had sent his family to England and had gone to live aboard one of the British ships under his command in the harbor at Yorktown.

"I still find the idea of our governor bearing arms against his own subjects a bit hard to believe," said Mr. Wentworth. Mr. Haskall was nodding as if he agreed.

"I'm afraid the reports are quite confirmed," said Mr. Peabody. "I talked to one of the unfortunate planters myself, a Mr. Trevallian. His entire tobacco crop and all of his outbuildings were burned. Needless to say, he is ruined, as are the other planters along the James who were targeted."

"Targeted?" said Mother, with an edge of concern in her voice. "That implies intent to single someone out, does it not?"

"Aye," Mr. Peabody answered soberly. "The plantations targeted for raids have all belonged . . . to Patriots."

# 3
## AN UNCOMMON HORSE

Felicity's heart gave a lurch. Patriot
plantations! Even though Grandfather
had been a Loyalist, Father supported the
Patriots, and everyone knew it. So that made
King's Creek a Patriot plantation, now that
Grandfather had left it in his will to Felicity's
family. If the king's soldiers under Dunmore's
command raided Patriot plantations along
the James River, what was to stop them from
coming north to the York—and to King's
Creek?

Felicity glanced at Mother. Mother's mouth
was a tight line. Felicity wondered whether
Mother was thinking the same thing she was.

"Well, then," sputtered Mrs. Wentworth,
"your Mr. Trevallian is obviously one of those

traitorous Patriots trying to stir up loyal subjects against the Crown!"

Felicity bristled. She had to bite her tongue to hold back the angry words she wanted to say to Mrs. Wentworth. The Merrimans were Patriots, but they weren't traitors!

There was an uncomfortable silence. All the adults, except Mrs. Wentworth, looked embarrassed. Finally Mr. Wentworth said to his wife, "My dear, you must remember that many of our neighbors have ... er ... shall we say"—he glanced at Mother, then at Mr. Peabody—"Patriot leanings."

Mrs. Wentworth squared her shoulders and sniffed, though she did offer what, for her, was an apology. "I meant no offense, you understand," she said, turning her head first to Mother, then to Mr. Peabody.

Mother and Mr. Peabody both nodded politely.

Mr. Haskall, a crease between his brows, looked thoughtful. "Mr. Peabody," he said, "I confess that I know little of your local politics, but I wonder if your governor feels that these planters are somehow harming the king's interests. After all, as the king's representative, he is sworn to honor his king above all else."

"Hear, hear," said Mr. Wentworth heartily. "I am certain that Lord Dunmore would not act in such a fashion against law-abiding citizens."

As if he had not heard Mr. Wentworth, Mr. Peabody said, his voice rising, "I fail to see how honoring the king requires destroying the property of his subjects."

"As some of us failed to see how destroying the property of the East India Tea Company honored the Patriot cause, in your so-called Boston Tea Party," Mr. Wentworth shot back.

Felicity noticed that the parts of Mr. Wentworth's ears that stuck out from below his wig were as red as one of Grandfather's apples. Mr. Wentworth was getting angry, as people so often did nowadays when they talked about the events of the last few years that had split the colonists into Loyalists and Patriots and ultimately led to war.

"Gentlemen," Mother said quietly but firmly, "perhaps these matters would be better discussed at another time."

"You're right, Mrs. Merriman. My apologies for bringing politics into your parlor," said Mr. Peabody.

"And mine as well," offered Mr. Wentworth.

"Well, I must take my leave," said Mr. Peabody. "I need to bring word of the raids to Lancaster Manor." The Lancasters owned a plantation downriver from King's Creek. Felicity wondered what their reaction would be to Mr. Peabody's news. Their eldest son, Richard, was with George Washington, fighting in the Patriot army.

"Good day, Mrs. Merriman, Mr. and Mrs. Wentworth," said Mr. Peabody with a slight bow. "Mr. Haskall, I trust you will call upon me again soon. I like a man who appreciates good horseflesh. Your father was such a man, Mrs. Merriman. We all miss him sorely."

"As do we," said Mother.

During the next few days, Felicity encountered Mr. Haskall as he gathered specimens on the plantation grounds or in the woods, once when she and Nan and William were gathering plums, another time when they were having a picnic under a beech tree, and again when they were cutting asparagus for Mother on the banks of King's Creek. He always had with him his large leather haversack to carry specimens and a leather-bound notebook in which he was often scribbling or sketching. Felicity liked the way he would stop his work to talk with them or show them interesting plants he had found.

About a week after Mr. Peabody's visit, Felicity took Penny out for an early-morning ride on the path that ran beside the pasture. The woods were a soft gray in the morning dimness. The sun was just coming up; the snatch of clouds she glimpsed through the trees was a light pink and the sky behind them dark blue, almost violet.

Felicity sucked in the delicious, cool morning air, so crisp and fragrant with the smell of pine. The birds poured out their morning songs, and honeysuckle bloomed along the trail in fluffs of white and yellow. It was just the kind of morning Grandfather would have loved, Felicity thought.

Felicity could tell that Penny was enjoying the morning, too. On the way home, she let Penny have her head. Penny fairly flew along the path. She sailed over a huge fallen tree that lay across the trail at the edge of the woods, then stretched out her neck and galloped into the open field beyond. There Felicity caught sight of Mr. Haskall, standing beside the pasture fence with his haversack slung over his shoulder, watching them. As they flew past him, Mr. Haskall applauded and shouted, "Good show!"

Felicity grinned. How she loved hearing people praise Penny! As they neared the stable, Felicity waved to Lester, who was standing in the stable doorway. When she began to rein Penny in, slowing her first to a trot, then to a walk, she was surprised to see Mr. Haskall hurrying toward them, his coattails flapping behind. "Miss Merriman!" he called. "Might I have a word with you?"

Felicity halted Penny and waited for him. "Yes, Mr. Haskall?" she said.

Breathless, he said, "I declare, I am quite impressed! Your mare bounded over that fallen tree trunk as if it were nothing but a twig. And now, after such a run, she's scarcely winded! She's a most extraordinary horse!"

Felicity felt a warm glow of pride. "Oh, yes," she said. "Penny's the finest horse in the whole world." She had reached the tree stump she used to dismount, and she slid off the sidesaddle and took hold of Penny's bridle to lead her to the stable.

Mr. Haskall patted Penny's withers, then held out his hand for her to smell. For a moment Penny's nostrils quivered as she sniffed him. Then, apparently approving, she stood quietly and let him rub her nose and scratch her neck.

"She likes you," Felicity said.

"Most people don't understand that a horse has to like your smell," Mr. Haskall said, "before she accepts you. May I walk along with you to the stable?"

"Of course," Felicity replied. As they walked, she told Mr. Haskall the story about how she had come to acquire Penny: how she had seen Penny, skittish and unkempt, being cruelly mistreated by her former owner, how she had secretly tamed Penny and set her free, and how, months later, Mr. Wentworth had acquired Penny in a swap and Grandfather had bought her from him for Felicity.

"For a long time Penny wouldn't let anyone else ride her save me," Felicity said. "Now, finally, she's learning to trust other people."

"Tell me more," said Mr. Haskall, his eyes alive with interest.

"I've a special way of calling her," Felicity went on. "If Penny is anywhere within earshot, she'll come at a gallop when she hears me."

Mr. Haskall's eyes lit up. "A special way of calling her? My grandpa's Sunday wig! What is it, Miss Merriman? I confess you have me intrigued."

"Well," Felicity said, a bit reluctantly, "'tis something Ben taught me—he's Father's apprentice back in Williamsburg—and 'tis not very ladylike. Mother wouldn't approve at all . . ."

"I'm very good at keeping secrets," Mr. Haskall promised. "I shan't breathe a word."

"'Tis a whistle," Felicity said. "I whistle to Penny in a certain way, and, wherever she is

35

or whatever she's doing, she comes running, for she knows I've a treat for her."

In a dramatic gesture, Mr. Haskall swept his tricornered hat off his head and bent in a bow. "I am your servant, Miss Merriman, amazed at your uncommon horse ... and her uncommon mistress."

# 4
## TROUBLE AT THE CREEK

The next day, Felicity, Nan, and William went fishing on the banks of King's Creek. When they fished, they didn't talk much. Instead they listened to the noises of the creek: the ripples and bubbles and sucking sounds as the water ran over and around green-lichened rocks, the screech of birds, the chirring of squirrels, the *kerplunk* of turtles sliding into the creek from sunny banks.

The fish weren't biting, so William gave up fishing and waded to the deep pools on the other side of the creek to sail a little pine-bark boat he had loaded with pebbles and grass. Nan was lost in her thoughts and Felicity in hers. Felicity, as she did anytime she got the chance, had removed her long white stockings and was soaking her bare feet in the creek.

Struck by the thought that Nan hadn't scolded her for taking off her stockings, Felicity glanced at her sister and smiled. It was nice the way she and Nan were growing closer now that Nan was older. This was the first summer they had really enjoyed spending time together, just the two of them. Then Felicity had another thought, one she knew would please her sister greatly.

"Nan," she said, "it won't be long before Patriot's ready to be halter-trained. Would you like to help me train him?"

Nan put down her fishing rod and beamed. "Oh, yes, Lissie, I would. When can we begin?"

Before Felicity could answer, she heard Mr. Haskall calling her name. She turned and saw him emerging from the woods. He wore a leather apron over his waistcoat and had his haversack slung over one shoulder. Striding toward them, he greeted Felicity and Nan warmly, his eyes gleaming with enthusiasm. "You'd be amazed at the extraordinary plant specimens I'm finding on your grounds and in your woods," he told them. Then he added, "That creek looks inviting. May I join you?"

"Of course," said Felicity. She loved hearing Mr. Haskall talk about his interest in plants. She was especially interested in what he had found on King's Creek land.

"What a prodigious hot day!" said Mr. Haskall as he sat down beside Felicity and Nan. He took his handkerchief from his waistcoat pocket and mopped his forehead with it. "I fear I shall never become accustomed to your Virginia climate." He gazed at William, splashing among the lily pads and weeds, and sighed. "I'm tempted to plunge into the stream, shoes and all, and wade as your brother is doing."

"But Mr. Haskall," Nan exclaimed, "you'd ruin your beautiful shoe buckles!" Mr. Haskall's shoe buckles were of the shiniest silver with tiny sparkling jewels encrusted in them.

"Ah," said Mr. Haskall, placing a hand over his heart with mock seriousness, "if only I could, I would gladly trade these shoe buckles for a return to the carefree days of my childhood."

Felicity and Nan laughed. Then Mr. Haskall let out a cry that made them both jump. "I say! What an excellent flower cluster on that specimen of *Nasturtium officinale*!"

Felicity glanced where he was pointing, to a clutch of white flowers on a water plant at the creek's edge. "You mean the watercress?"

"That is the common name, yes," he replied. He whipped a sketchbook and charcoal pencil out of his haversack and began sketching the flower. The girls leaned over to watch him.

William, always curious, waded over to see what his sisters were so interested in. "I like to draw, too," he told Mr. Haskall.

"Do you now, little man?" Mr. Haskall

stopped for a moment to ruffle William's hair. After a minute or two, William lost interest and splashed back out into the stream.

"He becomes bored quickly," Felicity apologized.

"Oh, yes, I understand," said Mr. Haskall. "I was a boy once too, you know."

Felicity watched Mr. Haskall's fingers fly across the foolscap paper as the drawing took shape, marveling at its likeness to the real flower. When he finished, he laid the sketchbook aside. "Now I must record where I found the watercress," he said.

Mr. Haskall pulled an ink bottle and quill pen and a leather-bound notebook out of his haversack, flipped through some pages in the notebook, and then, finding the page he wanted, dipped the pen in ink.

"King's Creek," he said thoughtfully, as he jotted the name and date at the top of the page. "A good naturalist always has his field notebook with him," he commented. "You see how many plants I already have catalogued in my notebook for your plantation. Here's my entry for snakeroot."

Felicity glanced at his notes about snakeroot, but Mr. Haskall, his eyes bright with eagerness, was already turning to another page. "And see here . . . creeping thyme." He flipped through more pages in quick succession, reading headings. "Beech drop, yew, leatherbark . . ."

Then he stopped and looked up at Felicity and Nan, pleasure showing on his face. "Yes, my young friends, the land on this plantation is as rich as Midas. Edible plants grow here in abundance, as do a number of trees and plants useful for cooking or for medicine. I'm certain a person could live off the land here in your woods for many weeks."

For a moment everyone fell silent. Nan went back to her fishing, but Felicity, with a pang, thought how much Mr. Haskall sounded like Grandfather. She had never seen anyone else take such delight in nature. "Grandfather used to say the same thing," she told

Mr. Haskall. "In fact, he used to tell me stories about his living in the woods when he was young."

She went on to tell him how Grandfather would point out useful plants to her on their rides about the plantation. "Once when Penny's leg was hurt, Grandfather showed me a plant I could use to make a healing salve for her. The salve worked beautifully."

"Ah," said Mr. Haskall with a happy sigh, "'tis a grand thing, is it not, the way nature provides us with everything we need, if we but know where to find it and how to use it? 'Tis why I like to study the natural world."

He told Felicity that he had made wonderful discoveries on Mr. Peabody's plantation, Rock Springs Farm, as well.

"What have you found?" she asked eagerly.

"Far more than I could begin to tell you," Mr. Haskall said. "And I've great expectations for the Lancasters' land as well, which I shall begin exploring very shortly, when I've finished with King's Creek."

"And what about the Wentworths?" Felicity asked. "Have you found interesting plants on their land?"

"The Wentworths have been most helpful," Mr. Haskall said. "Mr. Wentworth has been kind enough to allow me the use of one of his outbuildings—I believe it once was a laundry—for drying and storing my specimens and storing the equipment I use in my work." He invited Felicity to come the following day to see his workshop in the old laundry. "I'll be preserving the specimens I've found today. As a fellow nature lover, I think you'll find it intriguing."

"I'd love to," said Felicity, "if Mother will let me—"

Suddenly William screamed. "Arghh! Stop it! Get away from me! Ouch! Ouch!"

Felicity jerked her attention to William, a short distance downstream on the opposite creek bank. He was hopping, wailing, and waving his hands as a wreath of angry black insects swarmed around his arms.

"Hornets!" Felicity exclaimed, jumping to her feet.

"They're stinging William!" Nan cried.

"Stay here!" said Mr. Haskall. In a few long strides, he crossed the creek. He rushed to William, swept him up, dashed back across the water, and deposited the sobbing boy into Felicity's arms. "There. Safe and sound," he said. "The hornets won't bother you here, William. You must have disturbed their nest. Hornets rarely attack people otherwise."

"William, dear, are you quite all right?" Felicity asked him.

Nan was kneeling beside him, hugging him. "You must be more careful, dear," she crooned, in a motherly tone that made Felicity think again how grown-up Nan was getting to be.

"I hurt," William whimpered, sniffling and swiping at his runny nose with a wet muddy sleeve. "My hands." He held them up, and Felicity and Nan winced at the large red welts rising on his fingers and the backs of his hands.

"Let me see, little man," Mr. Haskall said. He took William's small chubby hands in his large ones. "Yes, you've gotten some stings. We'll take care of those right away."

He released William's hands and went to an area of the creek bank where tall weeds grew. He pushed into the weeds and came back a few moments later carrying several stalks of white-petaled flowers.

"Ooh, those daisies smell terrible," said Nan, wrinkling her nose.

"They're not daisies," Mr. Haskall said as he tore leaves off the stalks. "They are *Anthemis cotula*—otherwise known as dog fennel. A foul odor, to be sure, but wonderful for insect stings." He rubbed juice from the leaves on the welts on William's hands. "Does that feel better, my boy?"

William's face lit up. "It don't hurt a bit now!"

"Excellent!" Mr. Haskall said. "The swelling should be gone as well in an hour or so. The welts may still itch, but you mustn't scratch them, understand? They'll heal much faster if you don't."

"I won't scratch, I promise," William said with an earnest bob of his head.

"Good show!" said Mr. Haskall. "Would you young ladies like me to accompany you home and explain to your mother that William is in no danger?"

"Oh, no, that isn't necessary," said Felicity. "But thank you just the same." Then she glanced down at his shoes, dripping wet and muddy. "Mr. Haskall, I'm so sorry about your shoes."

"Pshaw, they needed a good wash anyway," said Mr. Haskall. Felicity knew it wasn't true. His shoe buckles had been spotless and gleaming before he went into the creek after William. "I trust, then, that you'll be coming to visit me tomorrow in my workshop, Miss Merriman?"

"Oh, yes," Felicity said. "After Mother hears how you saved William today, I'm sure she'll be happy to let me come."

"Good," said Mr. Haskall with a smile. "I shall look forward to seeing you then."

Nan looked at Mr. Haskall hopefully. "May I come, too?" she asked.

"Why, certainly," he said. "If your mother consents."

# 5
## THE OLD LAUNDRY

As it turned out, Mother didn't allow Nan to go with Felicity to visit Mr. Haskall's workshop. Nan didn't ride well yet, and Mother wouldn't let the girls go by rowboat on the river so far alone. Nan was terribly disappointed.

"You shall come with me another time, dear," Felicity promised, "once we've finished your riding lessons." Felicity had just begun teaching Nan to ride Sophie, the most docile horse in the stable.

So Felicity rode Penny the five miles to Oak Hill, the Wentworths' plantation. Robert, a stableboy who usually accompanied her on her rides, came along. The Wentworths' house was situated about a quarter mile from the public road, up a lane shaded by oak trees. After leaving Penny with Robert at the Wentworths' stables, Felicity went around behind the stables, where a walkway led through a gate and down a hill to more outbuildings. She recognized the old laundry building by the huge iron pots outside. Mr. Haskall greeted her as she climbed the stone steps up to the building.

As he showed her around, she agreed that the old laundry made a wonderful naturalist's workroom. It had a huge brick fireplace inside where Mr. Haskall could dry plants. Rows of shelves and bins lined the walls. Some shelves were filled with pots, jugs, and bottles and some with books, and the bins held bulky specimens like roots and bark. From the eaves hung bunches of dried flowers. There were also several large wooden tables stacked with books and files and plant presses, and in an alcove in a corner, Mr. Haskall had placed a writing desk. On a shelf above the desk was a row of notebooks labeled with the names of nearby plantations.

"Are these your field notebooks?" Felicity asked, remembering the notebook he'd written in yesterday at the creek.

"Yes," Mr. Haskall replied, glancing up to see what she was referring to. He had been examining and sorting leaves and twigs from a pile on a table. "I've created a notebook for each of the plantations where I've done explorations. In them are my notes about the plants I've found, where each grew, and so forth. Like a journal of sorts." He picked up a magnifying glass and peered through it at a twig with bumpy bark. "Hmm. I wonder if this is *Fraxinus caroliniana*." Then, without looking up, he said to Felicity, "Have you ever kept a journal, Miss Merriman?"

"Yes, yes, I have," said Felicity. "Miss Manderly, who teaches me my lessons back in Williamsburg, gave each of her students a beautiful book with blank pages to use as a journal to help us practice our handwriting. Though I haven't always been faithful about writing in it every day," she confessed.

"Ah," he said. "You should. 'Twill give you a record of yourself at this age that you'll enjoy reading later." He held the twig he'd been looking at between his forefinger and thumb, drumming the table with the fingers of his other hand. "I simply don't know about this one. I shall have to go back and check. Could very well be *Quercus laevis.* Oh, well." He pursed his lips, then put the twig aside and picked up a leaf to examine under the glass.

Felicity was becoming accustomed to Mr. Haskall's bouts of deep concentration on his work. She was often the same way when she was engrossed in working with Penny and Patriot. She knew he would soon turn his attention back to her.

While she was waiting, she ran her fingers over the spines of the field notebooks on his shelf, silently reading off the names he had printed on them: Rock Springs Farm, Cedardale, and Marsden Grove. The latter two were plantations upriver from King's Creek. She didn't see the notebook for King's Creek, or one for Oak Hill, the Wentworths' plantation. She asked Mr. Haskall about it.

"Oh, there's a method to my madness, I assure you," said Mr. Haskall, putting down the magnifying glass and striding over to stand beside Felicity at the bookshelf. "These three notebooks are shelved," he said, with one hand placed on the tops of the notebooks, "because I've completed my documentation on the plantations. I've just begun to explore your grounds, so, of course, I've not yet shelved that notebook."

"And Oak Hill?" Felicity asked.

"I haven't a notebook for Oak Hill, either," he replied.

Felicity nodded. Of course Mr. Haskall would study Oak Hill last, at his leisure, since he was staying here with the Wentworths.

He stood at the bookshelf, his hand still on top of the notebooks. "Are there other questions I can answer for you about the notebooks, Miss Merriman?"

Felicity liked the way Mr. Haskall was always so eager to answer her questions. So many adults didn't seem to care much what children were curious about. "You must have a great deal of information in so many notebooks," she said. "What will you do with it all when you're finished?"

"I hope to publish my findings, as the Bartrams have done," he said. The Bartrams, he explained, were noted naturalists whom he greatly admired. "I want to write a book eventually. So you see why my record keeping must be precise."

"A book!" said Felicity. "How grand! Will you include King's Creek Plantation in your book?"

"Naturally," said Mr. Haskall with a smile. "But let me show you the pride of my laboratory, Miss Merriman—my collection of your rare native plants." He directed Felicity over to a large wooden case with compartments. The compartments were labeled and filled with an assortment of leaves, bark, flowers, and twigs. As Mr. Haskall talked about the specimens he had gathered and preserved, Felicity marveled aloud at how much he seemed to know about rare plants native to Virginia.

"Oh, yes," he said. "I've done extensive reading on the Bartrams' explorations of the southern regions."

Then he showed her his plant presses—rectangular boards fastened together with iron clamps—and explained that he used the presses for drying leaves, herbs, and flowers. He showed her how he labeled and catalogued the finished specimens. Felicity was amazed at how the pressed flowers maintained their brilliant colors. "Why, they look as if they had bloomed yesterday," she said. "However do you do it?"

"I'll show you," he said. He demonstrated how he flattened and arranged the flowers and leaves on blotting paper, laid them in the press, and tightened it. Gradually, he explained, the moisture would be squeezed out of the plants, and they would be perfectly preserved.

"My sister and I grew up on a farm in Pennsylvania," he told her as he worked. "Wildflowers grew in profusion in the fields and woods, and we would gather them by the armful, then press them between flat stones to preserve them. I, being of a scientific bent, would classify and catalog them in scrapbooks. She was the artistic one, and would use the pressed flowers to decorate sheets of foolscap. Then she would write poems or letters upon the foolscap. Perhaps you would enjoy doing the same thing."

"Yes, I would!" said Felicity.

"Then you may have one of these presses," he said, handing her an empty press from a boxful. "And I have a favor to ask of you in return. I need to go into Yorktown to send some of my plant samples to an apothecary friend of mine in Philadelphia, yet I hate to take a full day away from my explorations in order to make the trip. I understand that there is a path somewhere on King's Creek land that is a shortcut to Yorktown, more direct than the public road. You must know of the path. I was wondering if you could show it to me."

"Of course," said Felicity. "I'd be happy to. I'm certain Mother won't mind. We may do it tomorrow, if you like, early. I could show you the sun coming up over the river. Grandfather and I often watched the sunrise there. 'Tis a beautiful sight."

"Splendid!" said Mr. Haskall. "Why don't we meet at the stable? You could show me around there a little more thoroughly. I'd love to hear more about your grandfather's horses. Mr. Peabody praised them so highly."

Felicity agreed. Then she asked him if he had heard any more about Mr. Peabody's mare Midnight. Mr. Haskall said that, as far as he knew, Midnight was still missing.

"Oh," said Felicity, disappointed. "I was hoping that by now Midnight might have been found."

"Indeed." Mr. Haskall's face was sober. "You know, Miss Merriman, I believe—and I think you do, too—that there are certain horses that bond instantly with certain people. Midnight was such a horse, and I such a person."

Felicity felt a thrill go through her. "That's exactly how it was with Penny and me! Even though Jiggy Nye owned Penny, I felt a bond with her the moment our eyes met. But why do you say 'was,' Mr. Haskall? You talk about Midnight in the past tense, as if... well... as if she's gone forever." Felicity wasn't sure why that distressed her so much. Maybe it was because she had once lost Penny, when Felicity helped Penny escape from Jiggy Nye. Yet Felicity had always believed that someday Penny would return to her.

"Did I say 'was'? I didn't mean to," said Mr. Haskall. "Of course we may yet hope that Midnight will be found."

There was a hollow ring to his voice that bothered Felicity. Though he said there was still hope that Midnight would be found, it didn't sound as if he really believed it. Felicity had the feeling that he was just saying it for her sake, and that made her sad for Mr. Haskall. Felicity couldn't imagine losing Penny and knowing she would never see her again.

# 6
# THE PATH TO YORKTOWN

The next morning, Felicity arrived at the stable before dawn, and Mr. Haskall was already there waiting for her, along with Robert. Mr. Haskall's mount was a large bay gelding named Eclipse. Felicity was wearing the green riding habit that Grandfather had given her. Mr. Haskall was dressed for riding as well, in a plain sleeveless waistcoat over a white shirt, and knee breeches.

Mr. Haskall tethered Eclipse to the fence and followed Felicity into the stable. It was dark inside, and warm after the nip of cool air outside. The only sound was the soft fluttering of nostrils as the horses slept, and the only light the dim morning twilight through the open stall windows.

Felicity didn't need light to guide Mr. Haskall down the center aisle to Penny's stall; she could have found it with her eyes closed. Penny's leather halter with its shiny brass nameplate was hanging beside the stall door. Felicity slipped the halter over her arm, then clicked open the stall door and went inside, with Mr. Haskall behind her.

Penny and Patriot were asleep in their thick bed of straw, Penny flat on her side and Patriot with his head resting on his mother's shoulder. When Felicity called to Penny, Penny waggled one ear and opened her eyes. Then Penny stretched and got to her feet. Patriot stirred, lifted his head, and, when he saw that his mama was up, scrambled to his feet, still wobbly with sleep. Felicity clucked to Penny as she slipped on her halter and stroked her sleek neck. Penny nuzzled Felicity's arm.

"'Tis easy to see the bond of friendship between you and Penny," Mr. Haskall said softly, reaching over Felicity's shoulder to scratch Penny's muzzle.

Felicity smiled, happy that what she felt for Penny on the *inside* showed on the *outside*.

When Felicity began to saddle Penny, Patriot started moving restlessly around the stall, sensing that his mama was going somewhere without him. "He hates to be left behind," Felicity explained to Mr. Haskall, as she tightened the girth strap that secured the sidesaddle around Penny's belly.

"Can you blame him?" Mr. Haskall said. "Who likes to be left out when there's fun to be had? Perhaps it would help if you gave the little fellow a bite to eat to keep him occupied."

So Felicity fetched some hay from the loft and put it into the low hayrack in the corner of the stall. Patriot dropped his nose and sniffed the hay, then snatched up a mouthful and gleefully began chewing. He looked up but didn't stop eating even when Felicity led Penny away from the stall.

Soon the three of them were on their way to the river: Felicity on Penny, Mr. Haskall on

Eclipse, and Robert on Sophie. They rode by fields of green tobacco and corn, to the river, slate gray and cloaked in mist. To the east and across the river, the dark forest rose, a black silhouette with a halo of pink above the trees. As Felicity and Mr. Haskall watched in silence, the rim of the sun appeared, and, little by little, the sun slid up from behind the trees, a large yellow lozenge that turned the river to a shimmering silver shield.

Then they went on their way, edging the river and the fields, where the sun already felt warm, and into the cool of the woods. A breeze whispered through the pines and carried on it the smell of flowers and warm earth. It was so calm and peaceful in the woods, it made Felicity feel that way inside.

Mr. Haskall had suggested that they keep the horses to a walk. "So that I can remember the way," he said. Felicity noticed that he looked very carefully at everything they passed. He also didn't want to talk.

"I need to concentrate," he explained, "on

noticing landmarks. It would not do for me to lose my way the first time I try to go it alone. If I'm careful to *notice* things," he went on, "my memory serves me extremely well, almost like having a painting of them in my mind. Sometimes I can even sketch from memory, if I've taken care to *notice*."

"Such a memory must be useful in your work as a naturalist," commented Felicity.

Mr. Haskall laughed. "One would think. The trouble is, this poor brain of mine can only store a few mental paintings at a time. So if I don't record them all somewhere on paper, I'll soon forget. Hence my notebooks."

As they rode on, they fell into a companionable silence, Mr. Haskall turning his head this way and that to note his surroundings as they passed, and Felicity trying to see the familiar woods through his eyes. Robert was following a ways behind on the path. The horses seemed to sense that this was a time to be calm, and they fell into a contented walk, their heads bobbing up and down in rhythm to the thud of their hooves on the soft trail.

When they reached Philgate's Creek, Felicity pulled Penny to a halt and pointed across the swirling water to a footpath on the other side. "'Tis there, the path to Yorktown," she said.

"Ah," said Mr. Haskall, reining Eclipse to a stop also. "I'll take care, then, to notice my landmarks here. The black willow hanging over the bank there," he murmured, pointing to a tree with gray bark and leaves that drooped into the water. "And the way the bridle path makes a V here," he said, sweeping his hand to indicate the riding path that veered sharply back in the other direction. "And that rock formation," he added, bobbing his chin toward an oddly shaped boulder jutting out from the opposite bank.

"Now," he said with a chuckle, "I've canvas and colors for my mental paintbrush to do its work."

"I hope it will be a masterpiece then," Felicity said, laughing with him.

After that, they let their horses drink from the stream, and they talked while the horses grazed at the ends of their reins and Robert stretched out for a nap. Mr. Haskall was easy to talk to. Felicity found herself talking about the early days of her friendship with Penny, telling Mr. Haskall how she had disobeyed her parents to slip out at night and go to Jiggy Nye's tannery to see Penny, and then to train her, and eventually to help her make an escape.

"Both Mother and Father agreed that Jiggy Nye was mistreating Penny," said Felicity, "but they said neither they nor I could interfere, because Penny belonged to him. Even though I knew it was wrong to disobey them, I didn't feel that what I did for Penny was wrong. Caring about her the way I did, I believed it was the only thing I *could* do. I know that doesn't make sense..."

"It makes perfect sense," said Mr. Haskall. "Loyalty is complex, Miss Merriman. Some-times a person may feel loyalty to two people or ideals that are opposed to one another. And then a decision must be made about which of the two should come first, and often there is regret that one must be forsaken for the other.

"Your parents insisted that you must not interfere with Jiggy Nye's treatment of his horse, for the horse belonged to him. Yet *you* felt an obligation to Penny, who had become your friend. You disobeyed your parents in order to honor what you considered a more urgent calling—to save Penny's life. That didn't mean you no longer honored your mother and father. Neither did it mean you didn't respect their authority or the reasons they would have disagreed with what you did. Do you see what I'm saying?"

Felicity felt too full of emotion to speak. All she could do was nod.

"And yet," he went on, with a serious expression on his face, "perhaps you were even a bit dishonest with them—"

"I would never be dishonest!" Felicity broke in. Penny's head came up at the rise in Felicity's voice; then she went back to her grazing when Felicity said, more quietly, "I wouldn't be dishonest, Mr. Haskall. Mother has taught us to be true as the Gospel, always."

Mr. Haskall lightly touched Felicity's arm. "Oh, I don't mean really dishonest, Miss Merriman. Not where it counts." He placed a fist on his chest to indicate where his heart was. "But I imagine that at the very least you intentionally misled your parents, which is the same thing as lying, when you think about it. 'Tis often impossible to carry out secret plans without some dishonesty, is it not?"

Felicity felt a wave of guilt. She hadn't lied to her parents—not really—but it was true that she hadn't been entirely honest either. She had misled Mother about how she got her petticoats dirty. She had taken Ben's breeches without asking, and she hadn't spoken up when Mother asked him what had happened to them. She bit her lip. "I hadn't really thought about that part of it," she confessed.

"No doubt because it was painful to do so," he said gently. "'Tis painful to hurt or deceive those we care about." He paused a moment. She could almost see his thoughts working behind his forehead. He was searching, Felicity thought, for just the right words. She waited patiently.

He stroked Eclipse's withers, the white ruffles on his sleeve in stark contrast to the rich gleam of Eclipse's coat. At last he continued. "All things considered, you believed what you were doing for Penny was right in the end, and you were willing to risk a great deal, even your parents' anger, in order to help her. Do I understand you?"

"Yes!" Felicity exclaimed. "Yes. That's just the way it was."

They talked more after that, but Mr. Haskall's understanding words lodged themselves in Felicity's mind. She didn't think she would ever forget them.

Soon it was time to head home. They let the horses canter; even so, by the time they got back to the stable, the sun was sailing well above the treetops. Lester had turned all the horses out into the paddock. Mr. Haskall rode back to Oak Hill, and Felicity rubbed Penny down and gave her her morning oats. When she turned Penny out into the paddock, Patriot scampered toward his mother, nickering a greeting. Penny skimmed across the paddock toward him, the sunlight shining on her coat like flames.

Felicity leaned on the fence and watched them, thinking about her talk with Mr. Haskall. It was amazing the way Mr. Haskall understood her. She didn't think she had ever had a friend who had such a knack for putting Felicity's own thoughts and feelings into words. She was certainly glad she had had the chance to know him, and she would be sad when the time came for him to leave.

# 7
## INTRUDER IN THE STABLE

The weather the next day continued hot and sultry. By midmorning the air was already steamy. Both the front and back doors of the big house were kept open, but the breeze that blew through the entrance hall seemed nearly as hot as the kitchen fireplace. Felicity preferred to stay outside, where in the shade the heat was at least bearable.

Mrs. Merriman was to attend a tea that afternoon at the Wentworths'. Nan was going with her, but Felicity asked if she could stay home to work on her sampler.

"My, Lissie! This is indeed a surprise," said Mother, as she tucked a strand of Felicity's loose hair back under her white mob cap. "To what fortunate turn of events

71

do we owe this sudden interest in sewing?"
Mother well knew that Felicity hated the
tedium of sewing, particularly the elaborate
embroidery on her sampler.

In truth, Felicity would rather do anything
else than sit in a stuffy parlor on such a hot
day listening to Mrs. Wentworth chatter on
and on. Of course, she couldn't tell Mother
*that*. But since Mother was always after
Felicity to improve her stitches, she imagined
Mother would be delighted that she wanted
to practice on her own.

"Oh, Mother, I want to be out-of-doors,"
Felicity said. "I thought I could sit on the
bench in the garden under the cherry tree.
My fingers don't mind sewing nearly so much
if my eyes and ears and nose can be busy
looking and listening and smelling."

"I don't imagine your tongue will be busy
tasting the ripe cherries," Mother said,
her eyes twinkling.

"Perhaps only a few," admitted Felicity
with a smile.

Mother laughed. "You may stay, then. But I trust there will be no cherry stains on your sampler." Felicity promised to be careful.

After dinner Mother and Nan left in the carriage for Oak Hill, and Felicity settled herself in the shade of the cherry tree to sew. The garden was in full bloom. Bees hummed over the borders of white lilies and blue violets, poppies, roses, and snowball flowers. Warblers twittered in the fruit trees, and a catbird meowed from the hedge of currant bushes. The hot sun poured down golden as butter.

The day was so warm and the perfume of the flowers so sweet, Felicity's eyelids soon began to droop. Try as she might, she could not sew a stitch; it was a struggle just to stay awake. So she decided to put aside her sewing for a while and take Penny out for a ride. A canter through the cool woods, she thought, would be just the thing to revive her so she could come back and tend to her sewing.

Leaving her sampler on the bench, Felicity stole around the side of the house to the stable. It had rained earlier in the morning, so the horses had not been turned out to pasture. Inside the stable, the air was cool and dark and heavy with the sweet smell of hay and dung. As she came in and closed the door, the horses poked their heads over the stall doors, their ears pricked forward.

Felicity started down the aisle toward Penny's stall, the last one at the far end of the stable, greeting all the other horses by name as she passed them. As she neared Penny's stall, Felicity stopped short. The stall door stood ajar.

*How could the stable boys be so careless?* she thought, irritated. Then she remembered that the stable boys were working in the field today. Lester would have cared for the horses this morning, and he would never leave a stall door open. Felicity looked around for Lester to ask him about it, but he was nowhere in sight.

Then she noticed that Penny was acting strangely, too. Instead of nickering a greeting, Penny was stamping and snorting and twitching her ears, as if she was nervous about something.

"What is it, Penny? What's wrong?" Felicity asked, easing toward her. Felicity cocked her head, her senses suddenly alert. She had heard something from inside the stall—the clink of metal and the rustle and creak of movement.

Was someone in Penny's stall?

"Who's there?" Felicity asked. She waited, poker-stiff, listening, for what seemed an eternity.

Then came the soft scuff of shoes across hay, and out of the stall stepped Mr. Haskall, a lead shank draped over one arm. "Why, Miss Merriman, good day. I wasn't expecting to see you here. Your mother said you'd be occupied, sewing a sampler, I believe? Otherwise, I'd have asked your permission as well as hers to take Penny out for a ride."

Felicity's heart was still beating so hard with surprise that for a moment she couldn't reply. Relief flooded through her at finding only Mr. Haskall, and not some thieving scoundrel like the person who had taken Midnight. At the same time, she couldn't help feeling annoyed with Mother. Finally she blurted, "Mother gave you permission to ride Penny?"

*What had Mother been thinking?* Felicity wondered. She knew how skittish Penny could be with strangers. And besides, Penny was Felicity's horse. Mother shouldn't have given Mr. Haskall permission to ride Penny without asking Felicity first.

"Why, yes," Mr. Haskall said. "I spoke with her at the Wentworths', and she said, as you'd be occupied with your sewing, I might take this beautiful animal out for a quick ride. But, my dear girl, you've obviously come here to ride Penny yourself, so I'll just be going."

Felicity looked up at Mr. Haskall. She hoped her annoyance hadn't been too obvious.

"I *would* like to ride Penny," she told him, "but you could take Duchess, Grandfather's spotted mare." Felicity nodded toward Duchess's stall next to Penny's. "Duchess was the best horse Grandfather had until he bought Penny. If you like, we could ride together—"

"Oh, no, no, no," Mr. Haskall broke in. "'Tis kind of you to offer, but you needn't change your plans on my account." He bowed politely and gave Penny a final pat. "Enjoy your ride, Miss Merriman. We'll ride together another day."

After Mr. Haskall left, Felicity began cleaning out Penny's hooves and saddling her, all the while feeling a growing annoyance at Mother for giving Mr. Haskall permission to ride Penny. *Whatever had Mother been thinking?* Felicity decided to talk it over with Mother as soon as she returned from the tea.

Mother and Nan, though, didn't get home until nearly suppertime, so Felicity didn't have a chance to talk to Mother alone until she came up to Felicity's bedchamber to say good night. Felicity had already undressed for bed and was reading Grandfather's copy of *Robinson Crusoe* in bed by candlelight.

Mother came in and sat on the edge of the bed. Her shadow, thrown by the candle on the wall behind, trembled and jumped as the candle sputtered. As Felicity asked Mother about the day's events, Mother's expression grew puzzled.

"When I saw Mr. Haskall at Oak Hill," Mother said, "he did ask after you, though he didn't say a word about Penny. Perhaps he misinterpreted the permission I gave him to ride on our grounds, and that's why he thought he could take Penny for a ride."

"Oh," said Felicity. "That must be it."

Mother kissed Felicity and blew out the candle. "You should be flattered that Mr. Haskall thinks so much of your horse. Sleep well, my dear."

As Mother slipped quietly from the room,

Felicity gave a happy sigh. She had hated feeling so unsettled all afternoon. Now she felt better. It had all been a misunderstanding, nothing more. She fell asleep with a smile on her face.

# 8

## MR. HASKALL'S SECRET

The next morning when Felicity came
to breakfast, she was surprised to see Ben,
Father's apprentice, at the table. "I arrived
late last night, after you'd gone up to your
bedchamber," Ben told Felicity between bites
of the bacon and fried fish he had heaped
upon his plate.

"I'm surprised Mr. Merriman allowed
you to come," said Mother. "The store must
be very busy with delegates from the Virginia
Convention in town." She poured milk from
a little white pitcher into William's cup, only
half-full, because William usually spilled
more than he drank.

"Oh, yes," Ben said as he helped himself
to another wedge of hot cornbread from the

china platter in front of him. "Williamsburg is near bursting at the seams, and more delegates are arriving every day. That's why your husband sent me. He wished me to tell you that the store is so busy, he'll not be able to come for a visit as he'd planned. He's very sorry, Mrs. Merriman."

"Oh, dear." Mother's face fell. "We were so looking forward to his visit."

"I want to see Father," William wailed, his mouth, sticky with preserves, making an unhappy O.

"We haven't seen Father for weeks!" Nan protested.

Felicity, pierced by disappointment, said, "Father isn't coming at all?"

"He promises he'll come as soon as he can," said Ben.

"Well, then," said Mother, putting on a smile that looked forced, "we must make the best of the bargain. Tell us, Ben, is there other news from town? What of the convention?"

Ben's eyes glowed as he talked about the delegates from all over Virginia, gathered now in Williamsburg. They were discussing whether Virginia should support the colonies uniting together in rebellion against the kings.

"'Tis high time we freed ourselves from those British tyrants!" he said fiercely. "Do you know that Governor Dunmore's men have raided the plantations of some of the delegates? They've set fire to houses and buildings, burned crops, and killed sheep and cattle. Dunmore wants to punish Patriots, 'tis said, and keep Patriot crops and livestock from being used for our cause. What's more, they're taking for themselves some of the best horses from the plantations they raid—the no-good thieves." Ben's face was dark with anger.

"They've no right!" Felicity cried. To her, stealing horses was almost worse than burning crops and houses.

Mother shook her head. "'Tis a sad state of affairs when our former governor resorts to robbing his own people," she said quietly.

Ben clenched his fists on the table. "I can't wait for my birthday, so I may fight with the Patriot army!" Last summer Father had promised Ben that he could become a soldier when he turned eighteen, if he agreed to finish out his apprenticeship when he returned. Now Ben's eighteenth birthday was only months away. "By heaven, we'll show Dunmore who he trifles with!"

"If only I were a boy," Felicity burst out, "I'd go with you!" Then she glanced quickly at Mother, afraid that Mother would be angry with her for saying such a thing. She tried to explain. "'Tis only that I feel so useless, Mother, sitting idly by while the British mistreat us."

Mother sighed and touched an affectionate hand to Felicity's cheek. "My dear earnest daughter. You'll see one day that there is much we can do to fight injustice without taking up arms."

Later that morning, Felicity and Robert rode partway with Ben as he headed back to Williamsburg. Ben was riding Father's mare, Old Bess, and Felicity was on Penny. They made their way along the winding trail through thick pines and hardwoods, sunlight slanting through the leaves into patterns on the ground. As they rode, they exchanged news, Ben telling Felicity about a British spy who had been discovered in Williamsburg, and Felicity telling Ben about her new friend Mr. Haskall and his work as a naturalist.

Their horses were going at a long, swinging trot when they burst out of the trees into a clearing beside Philgate's Creek and came upon Mr. Haskall himself. He was sitting on a lichen-covered rock by the creek, writing in his notebook. He looked up as they approached and waved at them. He put the notebook into his haversack and got to his feet as Felicity and Ben pulled their horses to a halt in front of him.

Mr. Haskall, loosening the cravat around his neck, smiled up at Felicity on Penny's back. "Miss Merriman, this is an unexpected pleasure. And is this young gentleman a friend of yours?"

"This is Ben Davidson, Mr. Haskall," said Felicity. "He's an apprentice in Father's store in Williamsburg. Remember I told you about him? He's the one who taught me to whistle." She turned to Ben. "Ben, this is Mr. Haskall, the Wentworths' guest who is visiting Virginia for the first time."

"Ah, Mr. Davidson," Mr. Haskall said, holding out a hand to greet Ben, "you're the whistler. And Miss Merriman's friend besides. I'm sure, then, that we'll be friends as well. How do you do?"

Ben studied Mr. Haskall through narrowed eyes. Then he bent down from Old Bess to shake Mr. Haskall's hand. "How do you do, sir," he said in a chilly tone. "You say you're new to Virginia?"

Felicity looked at Ben sharply. Even though Ben was shy, he was always warm and friendly to the customers in the store. Why was he being so cool to Mr. Haskall?

Mr. Haskall didn't seem to notice Ben's coolness. He explained that he was visiting on his way from Philadelphia to South Carolina. "I am greatly enjoying the opportunity to study the flora of this fair colony," he added. "And since I have much yet this morning to accomplish elsewhere, I'd best be on my way. I bid you both good day, my young friends." He touched his hand to his hat and ambled down the path back the way Felicity and Ben had come.

Felicity turned to Ben. "I think my grandfather would have been pleased to think of Mr. Haskall studying the plants on our land. Don't you, Ben?"

For a moment or two, Ben didn't answer. The only sound was the birdsong and noisy squirrels, and the *crunch, crunch* made by the horses as they grazed.

"Hmmph," said Ben finally, frowning.

Felicity lost her temper. "Ben Davidson! I wish you would tell me why you're being so peevish!"

Ben scratched Old Bess between the ears. "I'm not being peevish," he said. "I'm thinking."

"About what?" Felicity asked.

Ben only shook his head. "Let's go on a bit farther. Then I'll tell you."

They pulled their horses into a walk, Robert riding a short distance behind Felicity and Ben. As they moved down the path, the cool shade of the woods closed in around them. The horses' hooves made soft sounds in the pine needles on the trail. There was the low ripple of the stream beyond the trees, the creak of leather and the clink of bits, but Ben was silent. Felicity started to grow impatient. "Ben—" she began.

"I've seen that man before," Ben broke in.

"Mr. Haskall?" Felicity said. "I don't see how you could have. He only arrived at the Wentworths' from Pennsylvania a few weeks ago, and you've been in Williamsburg."

Ben's chin came up. "I *know* I recognize him, Lissie. I can't place him, though."

All of a sudden, Felicity remembered her own first impression of Mr. Haskall. "That's strange, Ben. I had the same feeling about him the first time I met him. That he was familiar."

Ben drew back on the reins in surprise, making Old Bess toss her head. "You did?"

"Yes," said Felicity, with a flicker of unease. "Later, when I found out he'd only just come to Virginia, I thought I must be mistaken, so I forgot it."

"Don't you think," Ben said, "'tis more than a coincidence that we both had the same impression?" He was silent for a long moment, his brow wrinkled in concentration. Then he fixed her with a steady gaze. "I could swear I've seen him in uniform—a British uniform. The soldiers who guarded Governor Dunmore in his palace used to come into the store quite a lot. We both must have seen him there, Lissie!"

Old Bess lurched forward at the rise in his voice, but Ben reined her back. "What

I would like to know," he went on, "is why Mr. Haskall is here visiting the Wentworths instead of aboard ship with the rest of Governor Dunmore's men."

Felicity swallowed hard. Mr. Haskall was her friend. She didn't want Ben's words to be true. "Perhaps he's no longer in the British army," she offered. "Perhaps he's left the governor's service and is simply visiting friends like the Wentworths before going to his sister's in Charles Town."

Yet even as she spoke, a question formed in her mind. *Then why would he have to pretend he'd never been to Virginia before?*

"And perhaps my name's Benjamin Franklin," scoffed Ben. "No, your friend Mr. Haskall is up to something. Watch him carefully, Lissie."

After Felicity and Ben parted, worry about his suspicions pinched at her as she rode back with Robert along the path toward home. She didn't want to believe Ben's idea that Mr. Haskall was one of Dunmore's men. She was so lost in thought, she didn't even chat with Robert as she usually did. When Penny abruptly tossed her head and whickered, Felicity looked up and saw Mr. Haskall sitting on the same lichen-covered rock by the creek, busily scribbling on a piece of foolscap paper.

Just then, Mr. Haskell glanced up and saw Felicity and Robert. He stuffed the foolscap into his haversack, slung the haversack to his back, and strode over to Felicity. He gave Penny a pat and said, "Why, Miss Merriman, how fine to see you twice in a morning. And especially *this* morning!" Robert nudged Sophie over to the stream to drink.

"Mr. Haskall," Felicity said. "You're still here? I thought you were in a hurry to get on with your work somewhere else."

A grin burst out on Mr. Haskall's face as if he couldn't hold it back another second, and his words tumbled out nearly on top of one another. "Oh, Miss Merriman, I have just made the most thrilling discovery. And I might have missed it if I hadn't come back here. 'Twas Providence, I tell you, that I did return, for I have just made the most important discovery of my career."

Before Felicity could ask him what it was, he had hurried on. "'Tis a copse of rare Franklin trees, discovered by William Bartram only a decade ago. Mr. Bartram believed the Franklin tree existed only in a very limited area on the banks of a creek in Georgia. But I have found it here. Here. On the banks of *your* creek. You should be very pleased, Miss Merriman. Very pleased indeed."

He was smiling so broadly, and his eyes shone with such pleasure, that Felicity couldn't help but feel excited herself. "That's wonderful!" she exclaimed. "You must have been sketching the trees when I rode up. I'd love to see the sketch, Mr. Haskall. May I? Or better yet, the trees themselves. Would you show them to me?"

Mr. Haskall seemed to consider her request, stroking Penny's shoulder. Penny acknowledged his touch with a snort but kept on eating.

Finally he drew a careful breath and said, "Oh, Miss Merriman, I'd love to show you. But the trees are on the other side of the creek, farther downstream, in a swampy, muddy area, quite inaccessible by horseback. And on foot . . . well . . . you'd ruin your gown, and your mother would be angry with me, I'm afraid.

"I'd be happy, though, to bring you some of the blooms from the trees. They're covered with beautiful white flowers. You could use the press I gave you to preserve them."

Felicity sighed. Her skirts always seemed to get in the way of what she wanted to do! "Yes," she said, trying to hide her disappointment, "please do bring me some."

"I shall certainly do so," said Mr. Haskall, giving Penny a gentle slap. "Now, if you'll excuse me, I must hurry back to my workshop at Oak Hill to record this find in my notebook. Before that mental picture fades."

He touched a hand to his head. "Good-bye, Miss Merriman." Then he spun on his heels and walked quickly away. For an instant, his shiny shoe buckles flashed in the sun before he rounded a bend and disappeared from view.

Felicity sat on Penny, staring after him. Something niggled at her brain, something that she couldn't quite catch hold of. Then all of a sudden, it struck her.

His shoe buckles.

If Mr. Haskall really had been walking in the swampy area where he said he'd discovered the Franklin trees, his shoes would have been wet and muddy, as they were the day he went into the creek to save William from the hornets. Yet his shoe buckles were shiny enough to reflect the sun. And, now that Felicity thought of it, there wasn't a bit of mud on his clothes either.

Felicity frowned. Had Mr. Haskall made up the story about the trees to cover up what he was really doing?

And just what *was* he doing?

Felicity thought back, straining to remember exactly what she'd seen when she rode up on Mr. Haskall. He had been sitting on the same rock where she'd seen him before, sketching something—but not the Franklin trees, because he said that he'd discovered them farther downstream. Then what?

"Something he didn't want me to see," Felicity said aloud.

Something else occurred to her. Hadn't he said he had to hurry back to Oak Hill to record the Franklin trees in his notebook? Yet she had never known him to be out in the field looking for plants without carrying his notebook in his haversack. "A good naturalist always has his notebook with him," he had said to her the day at the creek with William and Nan.

So why didn't he have his notebook with him now?

*He's up to something,* Ben had said. *Watch him carefully.*

Felicity frowned. What was Mr. Haskall up to?

A sudden gusty breeze stirred old dry leaves beside the path into a swirl. Penny swung her head toward the leaves, flicking her ears in interest. Felicity absently watched the leaves.

Then her eyes went wide as she remembered something else Ben had said, something he had mentioned only in passing. Yet it was something that would make the pieces of the puzzle about Mr. Haskall all fit into place.

Felicity's pulse started pounding, and her chest felt squeezed tight. What if it wasn't Mr. Haskall's naturalist work that really was most important to him?

What if he was using his work as a naturalist to hide his real interest—an interest that required him to roam about the countryside, familiarizing himself with the farms and woods, sketching things and making notes, without arousing anyone's suspicions . . .

What if Mr. Haskall really was a British spy?

# 9
## MAPS

A spy.

Felicity swallowed hard. She was aware of the wind swishing through the pine boughs, the scolding of a blue jay, the movement of Penny's shoulders as she dropped her head to snatch a mouthful of high yellow grass. And the quickening of her own heartbeat as the words rang in her head.

Her throat felt coated with sand, her lips dry as paper. She recalled Ben talking about raids on Patriot plantations.

What if Mr. Haskall *was* a spy, and he was planning a raid on King's Creek Plantation? In her mind's eye, Felicity pictured ruined buildings and blackened fields, soldiers in red coats driving her family from their house, taking horses from the stable . . .

The thought of it—and her own unwitting part in it—brought tears to her eyes. "*I* told Mr. Haskall we were Patriots," she said aloud. "I showed him about the plantation, and I led him on the paths through our woods. If anything happens to King's Creek, it will be all my fault!"

Penny, sensing Felicity's distress, tossed her head and whinnied, then blew loudly through her nostrils. The tears on Felicity's lashes spilled out and trickled down her cheek. She dashed at them with her sleeve and hardened her resolve. "All the more reason, then, that I should try to find out the truth about him now."

But how?

*His notebooks.* Mr. Haskall wrote down everything in his notebooks. If there was any clue to his being a spy, wouldn't his notebooks be the likeliest place to find it?

"Yes," Felicity murmured. "I'll have to get a look inside his notebook for King's Creek."

How to do it, though? She thought a minute, fingering the reins absently. "I'll go at dawn tomorrow to his workshop in the old laundry, before Mr. Haskall is up and about. Mother's accustomed to my early-morning rambles."

The next day before dawn, Felicity slipped out of the house, saddled up Penny, and set out alone for the Wentworths'. She didn't take the public road for fear of being seen, but the path through the woods seemed darker and spookier than ever before.

Fog nestled in the trees, floating in ghostly shapes across the trail, and the clopping of Penny's hooves echoed eerily through the gloom, sending nervous shivers down Felicity's spine. Even Penny seemed on edge, her sharp ears flicking at every moving shadow and rustling bush. When the quavering wail of a screech owl made Felicity's skin prickle, she leaned against Penny's neck and breathed in her warm horsey scent to boost her courage.

Felicity was glad when at last they came out of the woods and, across an orchard shrouded in mist, she spied the dark shapes of the Wentworths' outbuildings. The sun was just coming up, tingeing the clouds in shades of scarlet and lavender. Crows cawed overhead as Penny jogged through the orchard and came up to the old laundry building, where Felicity tethered her behind a grove of trees.

Felicity crept into the laundry. It was dark inside, and she had to wait a moment for her eyes to adjust. There were no windows, but a gray light filtered through the chinks in the logs and through the open door, allowing her to see dimly. As she scanned the room, her eyes fell upon a notebook lying open on a table. On the shelf above it were Mr. Haskall's field notebooks, six in all; surely one was the King's Creek notebook.

In the dim light, Felicity couldn't read the

labels Mr. Haskall had printed on the spines, so she hurriedly scooped up the notebooks, including the open one on the table, and carried them outside to examine. She dropped down on the stone steps, the notebooks in her lap, and glanced at the spine of the open notebook: *Rock Springs Farm,* it said in Mr. Haskall's small, spidery handwriting. The page that it had been open to was blank. Felicity turned a few more pages and saw that they were blank, too.

"That's odd," she murmured. "Mr. Haskall said he had found a lot of interesting plants on Mr. Peabody's land. Shouldn't this notebook be full?"

Puzzling over that question, she flipped backward, to the first page—a title page with "Rock Springs Farm" written at the top. Next came a few pages with sketches of plants and notes about them. Then there were those curious blank pages, and then another page with a drawing on it, a drawing that seemed to be . . . a map.

Felicity studied the map. In Mr. Haskall's tiny print, there were arrows drawn and instructions on how to get to Rock Springs Farm... from *King's Creek Plantation*. Why would Mr. Haskall draw a map of King's Creek in this notebook? It didn't make sense.

Then she remembered something. When she had asked Mr. Haskall about the notebooks the first time she was here, he had stood the entire time with his hand resting on top of the notebooks. *As if he was guarding them, trying to keep her from taking them off the shelf and looking at them.*

Why? What was inside these notebooks that he didn't want her to see?

Felicity shuffled through the other notebooks, reading the labels on their spines: Cedardale, Marsden Grove, Lancaster Manor, King's Creek.

Then suddenly it hit her. These were all Patriot plantations! What about the other nearby plantations, the ones that were Loyalist—like Riverscape, the plantation

next to Mr. Peabody's? And Oak Hill? Had
Mr. Haskall even now not finished exploring
the Wentworths' land?

It occurred to Felicity that Mr. Haskall
had never really *said* that he was exploring
Oak Hill. He had always skirted away
from questions about discoveries on the
Wentworths' land. She thought back to his
words about carrying out secret plans. *You
might at the very least intentionally mislead
people . . .*

Is that what he had been doing all along
with her? Misleading her? Deceiving her?
Pretending to be her friend so that he could
spy out King's Creek land? Felicity felt sick
with the thought. But the notebooks seemed
to point in that direction, didn't they?

Dread heavy inside her, she picked up the
King's Creek notebook and stared at it for a
moment. Its leather-bound cover felt cool to
her touch, and smooth. She ran her fingers
over the title Mr. Haskall had inked on the
label: *King's Creek Plantation.*

Three little words, with so much meaning for her. She'd spent every summer of her life in that house, on those grounds, in those woods. So many happy memories were centered there, especially memories of Grandfather. It was as dear to her as her own home in Williamsburg.

Emotion welled up inside her, making her throat ache. What would she find inside this notebook? Evidence that Mr. Haskall was indeed . . . a spy?

Holding her breath, she thumbed through the first few pages inside: a title page, then sketches and notes about plants. And then the same blank pages—page after page after page, all blank. Most of this notebook, too, was empty. She knew that Mr. Haskall had been many days exploring King's Creek land. If not looking for plants to record in this notebook, what had he spent his time doing?

She didn't want to answer that question.

The cold of the stone steps was seeping through her skirts to her skin, and her legs had begun to feel tingly from sitting so long in the same position. When she stretched her legs out to relieve the numbness, a sheet of loose foolscap slipped from between the blank pages of the notebook. Felicity snatched the paper up and looked at it.

It was another map, this time of only King's Creek Plantation. The map showed the big house and all the outbuildings on the plantation, as well as the fields and the surrounding woods, from King's Creek to Philgate's Creek, *with the footpath to Yorktown marked and identified.*

Felicity felt a clutch at her stomach. Was this a spy's map, a map that would lead Dunmore's soldiers from Yorktown through the woods straight to King's Creek Plantation?

Was that why Mr. Haskall had been so interested in the path to Yorktown? Not for him to use to go to Yorktown, but for British soldiers—Dunmore's men—to use to ride from Yorktown to King's Creek Plantation, so they could burn it to the ground? Had she, not knowing it, given Mr. Haskall and the British a tool to use against the Patriots— and her own family?

Her mind rocked, yet she knew that she shouldn't jump to conclusions, even if the conclusions fit her suspicions—and Ben's— about Mr. Haskall.

The map, she realized, didn't prove that Mr. Haskall was a spy. It didn't prove anything. It could well be an innocent map Mr. Haskall had made to help him find his way about the plantation, or to mark where he found his specimens. After all, he had said that he wanted to use the path she had shown him to take his specimens to Yorktown, so it made sense that the path would be marked and identified on his map.

Outside somewhere, a rooster crowed. Dawn was quickly broadening into day. Pressed with the need to hurry—any moment Mr. Haskall might come and find her here—Felicity jumped up and replaced the notebooks on the shelf.

As she turned to go, her eyes fell upon
Mr. Haskall's waistcoat hanging in an alcove
on a peg on the wall. Poking out from under
the waistcoat was his haversack. Yesterday
when she had come upon Mr. Haskall, he'd
been quick to stuff the paper he had been
writing on into his haversack. Maybe it was
still there.

Did she have time to search the haversack?

She glanced back inside the laundry. The
room was no longer dark. The rising sun
lanced through the gaps between the logs
and fell upon the neatly organized shelves
and tables inside. For one tense moment
she struggled, her fear of being discovered
battling with her fierce need to know the
truth about Mr. Haskall.

At last, her desire to know the truth won
out. Her stomach churning nervously, she
lifted the waistcoat and haversack off the peg,
rummaged through the haversack, and pulled
out Mr. Haskall's sketchbook. His story about
the Franklin trees came sharply to her mind,

so she flipped through the sketchbook, but its pages were empty. Obviously he hadn't been sketching yesterday. The only other things in the haversack were some empty specimen bottles, a charcoal pencil, and a lead shank matted with black horsehair.

For a moment Felicity fingered the lead shank. Why did Mr. Haskall have it in his haversack? A lead shank seemed a strange thing for a naturalist to carry with him out into the field . . .

Just then another rooster crowed outside, and Felicity's heart thumped. She had to hurry!

Hastily she closed up the haversack and replaced it on the peg, then hung up the waistcoat over it again. Turning to go, she noticed a corner of foolscap sticking out of the waistcoat pocket. The foolscap had writing on it, in large rounded letters, definitely not Mr. Haskall's handwriting.

Felicity fished the foolscap out of his pocket and looked at it. There was just one line: *Rendezvous Y 21 JN.*

*Rendezvous,* Felicity knew, meant "meeting" in French. The rest of the note didn't seem to make any sense at all.

Unless Mr. Haskall really was a spy.

And this note was a message written in code.

# 10
## RENDEZVOUS

Felicity swallowed hard. A coded message. If it was true, the note she held in her hand was meant to set up a meeting—a rendezvous—between Mr. Haskall and ... someone. Someone who wanted to keep their meeting a secret.

There wasn't time to puzzle now over the note. Already the sun was bright inside the laundry. Shining dust motes floated among the bunches of flowers and herbs hanging from the eaves. Soon it would be time for breakfast. If Felicity didn't show up to eat, Mother would be worried. Besides, every minute she lingered increased the risk that Mr. Haskall would come and find her here.

Felicity decided to take the note with her.

If Mr. Haskall missed it, she hoped he would think that he had dropped it somewhere. She stuffed the note into her apron pocket and hurried to untether Penny.

As soon as she was mounted, Felicity kneed Penny into a canter. As they flew across the orchard, Penny must have sensed Felicity's urgency—she asked for a free rein, and when Felicity gave it, Penny stretched out her neck and plunged into the woods at a gallop.

During breakfast, Felicity scarcely ate. All she could think about were the maps and the rendezvous note she had found in Mr. Haskall's workshop. Did they prove he was a spy? She wanted to tell Mother about Mr. Haskall, but she couldn't bring herself to do it. What if she were wrong?

At midmorning, Mrs. Wentworth came for coffee, and Mother, as usual, required Felicity to be present. They took coffee in the tearoom that opened into the dining room. The Merrimans, like most Patriot families, had stopped drinking imported tea to protest

England's heavy taxes on it. The three of them sat around the polished tea table, and Mother poured from the sterling silver coffee service that had belonged to *her* mother.

Felicity's worry over Mr. Haskall was like a lump in her throat. She couldn't drink her coffee or keep her mind on Mother's and Mrs. Wentworth's conversation. Instead, she stared out the tearoom's tall windows, where the sunlight streamed through the panes, making squares on the opposite wall. The slatted blinds stirred slightly in the breeze.

Outside she could see the formal garden with its border of poppies and phlox. A butterfly had lighted on a poppy, and Felicity watched the butterfly, its delicate yellow wings contrasting against the bright orange of the poppy.

Then she heard Mrs. Wentworth mention Mr. Haskall's name. Immediately she perked up her ears.

"We really hate to see him go," Mrs. Wentworth was saying. She took a sip of her coffee, then grimaced. "I confess I don't understand how anyone could actually prefer coffee to our king's good tea." Not only did the Wentworths still drink tea, but Mrs. Wentworth never seemed to miss an opportunity to express her disagreement about the Merrimans' decision *not* to.

Mother politely ignored Mrs. Wentworth's comment. "When will Mr. Haskall be leaving?" she asked. "Will you have another cake, Mrs. Wentworth?" Mother added, offering Mrs. Wentworth the tray of Banbury cakes and tea biscuits.

Mrs. Wentworth took the largest cake from the tray and placed it on her plate. "He sails from Yorktown tomorrow," she said. "I can't believe 'twill be the twenty-first of June already. How quickly his visit has flown by!"

*Mr. Haskall was heading for Yorktown on the twenty-first of June.*

The meaning of the note on the foolscap exploded in Felicity's mind like a keg of powder: The note was a message, setting up a meeting with Mr. Haskall on the twenty-first of June in Yorktown—the *Y* stood for Yorktown and the *JN* for June.

And the twenty-first of June was tomorrow!

# 11
## FELICITY'S PLAN

A knot tied itself tight in Felicity's stomach. The time for puzzling over what to do about Mr. Haskall had run out. Felicity excused herself from the table and hurried upstairs to her bedchamber. She flung herself down on on the chintz coverlet on her bed to think.

She was sure the meeting was somehow connected with all the other unexplained bits and pieces about Mr. Haskall that had been collecting in her mind like scattered parts of a puzzle: the notebooks about Patriot plantations, the blank pages, the maps, the shiny shoe buckles ...

Yet there seemed to be something lacking, an absent piece of the puzzle that kept the others from fitting snugly together.

"I'm missing something," Felicity whispered to herself. *What is it?*

She thought back over her search of the laundry, going over everything she had found and every action she had taken. Finally it came to her.

The lead shank she had found in Mr. Haskall's haversack had been matted with horsehair, black horsehair. That meant he had last used the lead shank on a black horse. Midnight, Mr. Peabody's missing mare, was jet-black.

Could Mr. Haskall have used the lead shank to steal Midnight?

Like chain lightning, another thought occurred to her, a thought so terrible, it made her skin prickle in gooseflesh. The day in the stable, when she had found Mr. Haskall in Penny's stall with a lead shank over his arm, had he been trying to steal *Penny*?

Felicity's head started spinning and a cold, sick feeling flooded her body. Was it true?

Would Mr. Haskall—her friend—take her horse and give her to the British army?

Felicity's heart began to thunder.

*The lead shank.*

The lead shank proved it, didn't it? Proved that Mr. Haskall had gone to the stable that day not to ride Penny, but to lead her away with him to one of Governor Dunmore's ships. Just as he had done with Midnight.

And he would have succeeded, if Felicity hadn't shown up. Once she had seen him there, he had known his plan to steal Penny was ruined. So he had hurried away before Felicity could figure out that something was amiss.

A tremor ran along Felicity's spine, like a trickle of cold water down her back.

Mr. Haskall was a spy!

Felicity knew now with sickening certainty why Mr. Haskall had placed the maps between blank pages in his field books: to conceal the maps from anyone who might happen to thumb through one of the notebooks.

The blank pages would make the person think that he had come to the end of the notes, and the person would turn no more pages. And the maps looked harmless enough anyway. Who would suspect that secret maps would be hidden in a naturalist's field book?

She was willing to bet that Mr. Haskall was planning on turning the maps over tomorrow to one of Dunmore's soldiers. Or to Lord Dunmore himself!

*So little time.*

Tomorrow Mr. Haskall would ride for Yorktown with the maps. Tomorrow he would meet the mystery person. And then Dunmore's soldiers could start their march toward King's Creek.

Fear began to curl itself around Felicity's spine like a big black snake. One day was all she had, one day to stop the raids on all the Patriot plantations along the York.

But what could she do in so little time?

Felicity buried her face in the crook of her arm and tried to think, but her brain seemed to be frozen. Not a single idea would come to her, and that made her even more frightened. Her heart was beating so hard, Felicity could feel it thumping in her chest.

This would never do. She had to calm herself and try to clear her head. She went to the window, wide open to let in the breeze, and leaned out over the sash. The sun hung high in the sky, burning through the summer haze. From here she could see all the way to the pasture behind the stable. There, with the other mares and foals, she saw Penny and Patriot.

The foals, Patriot among them, were galloping up and down the pasture, chasing each other. Penny was grazing quietly, her copper-brown hide so glossy and sleek that Felicity felt stunned by her beauty. Her throat swelled with love for her horse, and then an idea came to her, an idea that was both wonderful and terrible.

It was wonderful because Felicity felt sure it would work. It was terrible because it involved a huge risk. Her idea was a plan, a way to lay a trap for Mr. Haskall.

And Penny was the bait.

Felicity's mouth felt dry with dread as she thought about what would happen if her plan failed. She could lose Penny! But if she did nothing, her beloved plantation—and those of her Patriot neighbors—could be destroyed by British troops.

Yet, if the trap worked as she hoped, both Penny and the plantations would be safe. Felicity knew she had to try.

She paused a minute to think. Then she grabbed up a sheet of foolscap, a quill pen, and an inkpot from her writing table and jotted a message to Ben.

*Ben,*

*Mr. H. is a British spy! Found maps and coded message among his belongings. Have reason to believe message sets up meeting in Yorktown to turn over maps to British soldiers on June 21st (tomorrow).*

# FELICITY'S PLAN

*I have a plan to stop him but I need Father's help. You must convince Father to bring men and lie in wait for Mr. H. along footpath to Yorktown on Yorktown side of creek tomorrow. Mr. H. will be traveling path sometime after breakfast and will be carrying maps of King's Creek and other Patriot plantations. Ben, you must not fail to convince Father!*

*With utmost urgency,*
*Felicity*

She held the note up to read, blowing on it to dry the ink. There was something missing, something important. With fingers trembling, she added a final line: *P.S. Tell Father that Mr. H. will be riding Penny.*

Seeing the words in black and white, Felicity almost lost courage and tore the note up. She couldn't risk Penny! But if she didn't, she told herself, there would be no way to stop Mr. Haskall from delivering the maps of Patriot plantations to Lord Dunmore. And no way to stop Dunmore's men from raiding and burning those plantations.

"I have to do it," she whispered. "I have to." Swallowing the lump in her throat, she pulled the rendezvous note out of her pocket, lit a stick of sealing wax, and dripped wax from it onto the rendezvous note to fasten it to the message she had just written. With more wax, she sealed the message and marked the outside of it with Ben's name and the word *URGENT* in capital letters.

Now she had to write another note, this one to Mr. Haskall. She picked up the quill pen again, dipped it into the inkpot, and started writing.

*Mr. Haskall,* she began. *I have a great favor to ask of you.*

How her heart was pounding! She stopped, breathed, waited until her heartbeat slowed. Then she dipped the pen again and finished the letter.

> *I have come down with a prodigious bad sore throat, and my mother insists that*

*I stay in bed until I am better. This means that I will not be able to ride Penny! I am greatly distressed, knowing how much Penny will miss her morning jaunt. Would you consider taking Penny out for a ride tomorrow after breakfast? I know that you understand how important daily exercise is to a spirited horse like Penny. Your prompt reply will set my mind at ease.*

    *I am*

*Sincerely yours,*
*Felicity Merriman*

For a moment she sat and stared at the sealed messages. If she sent these messages, there would be no turning back. She would have to go ahead with the plan. She stared so long that the letters began to swim in front of her eyes.

Finally she closed her eyes and pressed the notes to her chest. She had to believe that everything would work out, that Ben would be able to convince Father to cooperate, that

Mr. Haskall would agree to ride Penny, and that Father would catch Mr. Haskall before he could make off with Penny. It was the only way she could make herself carry on with her plan.

Quickly, before she could change her mind, she snatched up the sealed sheets of foolscap and sailed down the stairs. She headed to the stable first and gave one message to Robert to deliver to Ben in Williamsburg. She gave the other message to Asa, one of the house-boys, to deliver to Mr. Haskall. She asked Asa to deliver the message directly into Mr. Haskall's hands and to wait for an answer. Then she went to her bedchamber to await Mr. Haskall's reply.

Time crept by. At one o'clock, Tildy came to call her to dinner, but Felicity told Tildy to tell Mother she wasn't hungry. Which was true—she was much too worried to think about eating. Through the long afternoon, Felicity tried to stay occupied in her room by practicing her penmanship, trying to form the letters in her copybook just as Miss Manderly had shown her. She wrote and rewrote the same rhyme: *When land is gone and money spent, Then learning is most excellent.*

With each repetition, her handwriting deteriorated. She simply couldn't keep her mind on her work. All she could think about was what Mr. Haskall would say in his reply. When she heard the clock downstairs strike five, she began to fear that something had gone wrong. Why hadn't Asa returned?

Just as Felicity was putting on her cap and straw hat to go look for Asa, there came a knock at her door. She rushed to open it. Asa stood outside in the hall, holding a silver tray with a sealed letter on it.

"Your reply, miss," said Asa.

"Oh, thank you!" Felicity cried. She took the letter from the tray and tore through the seal. Her eyes flew over the words, her lips moving silently as she read. Then she felt the blood drain from her face. "Oh, no," she said. "Oh, no."

"Miss Felicity!" Asa said, looking alarmed. "Are you ill?"

It was all Felicity could do to force herself to speak. "Yes, Asa, I am ill," she answered, her voice cracking. "I must go now." She stepped inside her chamber, shut the door, and leaned against it to keep her knees from buckling. She felt faint. In all her worrying about what could go wrong with her plan, she had never once considered what would happen if the *timing* of her plan went awry. And now it had.

In his note, Mr. Haskall *had* agreed to take Penny for a ride. But he said that he would have to come *at dawn,* not after breakfast as Felicity had asked.

Which meant he would be long gone with Penny before Father ever arrived.

# 12
## PURSUIT

Felicity pushed against the panic gathering in her chest. There must be some way to deal with this, some way to fix it so the plan would still work. She read Mr. Haskall's note again.

*Dear Miss Merriman,*

*I am most happy to assist you by exercising Penny tomorrow morning. However, as I am to sail from Yorktown by noon, I'll need to take her out at dawn rather than after breakfast as you suggested. I regret that I will not be able to say good-bye to you in person, and I do wish you a speedy recovery. I shall always remain*

*Your friend,*
*Mr. Haskall*

Bitterness rose in Felicity when she read Mr. Haskall's closing. He was anything but a friend! Angrily, she crumpled up the note. She knew what she would do, what she had to do. She would follow Mr. Haskall. If he got across the creek with Penny before Father arrived to stop him, she would just have to stop him herself, or at least delay him until Father could get there—though she didn't have the slightest idea how to do that.

"Somehow I'll do it," she whispered, her fists clenched. "Somehow."

Her thoughts were interrupted by a knock at the door and Nan's voice outside. "Lissie, may I come in?"

"Nan, I—" Felicity began.

The door was already opening and Nan's worried face peered in. "I was coming up the staircase, Lissie, and I heard you tell Asa that you're ill. What's wrong with you? Should I fetch Mother?"

Felicity started to reassure Nan that she was fine, but then, suddenly, she felt as if she had to share her burden with someone, if only a small part of it. So she pulled Nan into her chamber, sat with her on the bed, and, being careful not to alarm her sister, told Nan what she had discovered about Mr. Haskall.

When Felicity got to the part about her plan, and going out after Mr. Haskall and Penny herself, Nan exclaimed, "No, Lissie! Please don't do it. What if ... what if something should happen to you?"

"I don't think it will, Nan," Felicity said. "I don't think I have anything to fear from Mr. Haskall. But, just in case, if I don't come back by dinnertime, you're to tell Mother everything. Say nothing, though, until then. Do I have your word?"

Nan promised.

❧

That night Felicity went to bed as usual, but after Mother came in to say good night, she got back up. She had determined that she would sit up for the night in the wing chair by her window. That way she would sleep lightly and would be sure to hear the clock downstairs strike four—the hour before dawn. That was when she planned to go out to the stable to wait for Mr. Haskall. She sat wrapped in her coverlet because the night was cool, watching rain dribble down her window and listening to it drum on the roof.

She must have dozed off, because she was awakened by the soft *thump* of her door swinging open. Nan in her long white nightshift padded into Felicity's bedchamber. "Lissie," said Nan, "I couldn't sleep for worrying about you."

Felicity beckoned to her. "Then come and sit with me for a while." Nan hurried across the room and snuggled up next to Felicity in the chair. Felicity wrapped the coverlet around them both, and, for a long time, they sat together in silence, the only sounds the soft patter of rain and the *click-click* of a tree branch on the window. Finally Nan asked, in a small voice, "Lissie, must you go?"

Tenderly Felicity touched her knuckle to Nan's cheek. "You know I wouldn't do it if I didn't have to."

Nan gave a great sigh. "I wish I could go with you then."

"You'll be with me in thought," Felicity said, forcing a brightness into her voice that she didn't feel. "But there's something I need you to do for me, Nan. I may not be home for breakfast, so you must tell Mother that I rose early and went for a ride and took my breakfast with me. Will you do that?"

"All right, Lissie," Nan said. She hesitated. "I do hope Mother won't be angry with you, though."

Felicity knew how Nan worried about pleasing Mother. "Dear Nan," she said, "Mother won't be angry. She knows how I love my early-morning rides."

She hugged Nan close to her. Through Nan's thin shift, Felicity could feel the thumping of her sister's heart. Or was it her own? "Now off you go, back to your own bed. Say a little prayer for me, Nan, but then try to put it out of your mind until dinnertime. Otherwise you'll act unnatural, and Mother might suspect something."

Silently Nan slid out of the chair. Her nightshift, one Felicity had outgrown, swept the floor as she walked, making it seem as if she floated, like a ghost, to the doorway. There she stopped and turned and stared back at Felicity, her eyes dark pits in her pale face. "I'm so afraid for you," she said, "and for Penny."

Felicity swallowed. Inside, she felt as frightened as Nan, but she did her best not to let it show. "You mustn't be," she said. "You must believe everything will go according to plan. And it will. I promise." She only wished she were as confident as she sounded.

After Nan had left, Felicity didn't go back to sleep. Instead she sat thinking of Penny and Patriot. They would be sleeping now in their deep, clean bed of straw, unaware of the peril the morning might bring.

At last the clock struck four. The rain had stopped, though dark clouds drifted across the moon.

Felicity dressed quickly by moonlight. She had slept in her stays, knowing she couldn't lace them by herself. Carrying her shoes in her hands so as not to wake anyone, she skimmed in her stocking feet down the back stairs, put on her shoes, and went out into the night. A night wind sighed through the trees, and a sheet of mist floated over the grass. The pasture and paddock were a sea of mud.

Felicity slipped into the stable. It was shadowy and quiet except for the slow, sleepy breathing of the horses. Moonlight from the opened stall windows glinted off the brass rings beside each stall. She glided down the center aisle to an empty stall across from Penny's and flung herself down in the straw to wait for Mr. Haskall. As she lay listening to the scratching and rustling of mice in the loft above, her eyelids drooped, and she had to pinch herself to stay awake. The worst thing that could happen, she thought, would be to fall asleep and miss Mr. Haskall...

The next thing she knew, she jerked awake to the sound of a whinny and a male voice crooning, "Now, girl, ready to go."

*A dream*, her fuzzy brain told her. She started to slide back into sleep. Then came the *thump-thump* of a stall door opening and closing, and the clatter of hooves on the stone floor. Felicity's eyelids flew open. *Mr. Haskall had come to take Penny!*

She lurched to her feet and peered over the top of the stall door. In one dizzying instant she took it all in: Penny's stall door closed; Duchess's stall open, with the door swinging gently; the chink of a bit—it was Duchess's habit to bite at the bit; Mr. Haskall, his back turned, in his leather coat and white shirt; Duchess's broad, speckled haunches; the stable door rattling open and Mr. Haskall leading Duchess out; the door shutting with a *whack*.

# PURSUIT

Mr. Haskall was taking Duchess—not Penny!

Felicity shook her head. Was she still asleep, dreaming this? She flung herself up, shot across the aisle to Penny's stall, and glanced inside. It was real! Penny and Patriot were there, sound asleep and safe.

Why had Mr. Haskall taken Duchess instead of Penny?

Felicity ran to the stable door and pressed her ear against it. Outside she heard whinnies and snorts—from two horses, she was sure— and the mumbled sound of Mr. Haskall's voice, talking to the horses, she supposed. She strained to pick up what he was saying. She couldn't make anything out, except Duchess's name and the name of Mr. Haskall's horse, Eclipse. Duchess and Eclipse must be the two horses she was hearing. Then she heard the *thud* of hooves. They were leaving!

She slid the stable door open a crack and saw Mr. Haskall on Eclipse, his haversack and a leather luggage bag tied to the saddle.

They galloped into the shadowy woods, with Duchess in tow.

Felicity stood, frozen. Now she knew that it was true—Mr. Haskall *was* a spy. He had stolen Duchess, one of the most valuable horses in King Creek's stable, for the British army. And the haversack surely contained the maps of Patriot plantations.

*But he hadn't taken Penny.*

Felicity felt a rush of relief—and then she felt ashamed of herself. How could she be relieved when Mr. Haskall had made off with Grandfather's prize mare?

"Because it proves he really was my friend," she whispered. "He could have taken Penny, but he didn't."

Still, misery squeezed her chest tight. Friend or not, she knew Mr. Haskall had to be stopped. At this very moment, he was on his way to Yorktown to hand over to the British his maps of King's Creek and the other Patriot plantations along the York. And Father wouldn't be waiting for him on the other side of the creek until *after* breakfast—hours from now. *If* Ben had even been able to convince Father to go.

So there was no one to stop Mr. Haskall but Felicity. She had to wake up Penny and go after him. Maybe, if she caught up with him, she could change his mind, convince him not to give the maps to the British. But she had to hurry. Yorktown wasn't far. A swift horse could be there in an hour.

But Eclipse was slowed by Duchess. Penny would be much faster.

Soon Felicity was on Penny, galloping through the woods on the path toward Philgate's Creek and the cutoff to Yorktown. The tracks of Eclipse and Duchess were easy enough to follow in the soft earth. The woods were silvery gray in the thin dawn light, and fragrant with the smell of rain-washed air. Felicity took little notice of the woods or the air. All she could think about was catching up with Mr. Haskall.

When Felicity glimpsed the creek ahead,

its water dark and silent, she urged Penny forward, up, and across. Penny sailed over the creek and broke into a gallop on the opposite bank. Small stones along the path sprayed up from her flying hooves. Girl and horse flew through the woods, Felicity pressing against Penny's straining neck, while the trees rushed by on either side.

At last, as Penny pounded around a bend in the path, Felicity saw Mr. Haskall, Eclipse, and Duchess far up ahead of them. At the same moment *she* spotted *him*, Mr. Haskall turned in the saddle and spotted Felicity and Penny. Before Felicity realized what was happening, he had reined Eclipse in, snatched up the haversack, leaped from Eclipse's back, and darted into the forest on foot.

# 13
## BETRAYAL

At the spot where Mr. Haskall had disappeared into the trees, Felicity pulled Penny abruptly to a halt and scanned the woods, but she saw no sign of him. Eclipse and Duchess stood idly, snatching mouthfuls of grass alongside the path. They swung their heads up and whinnied a greeting to Penny. Penny returned the greeting.

Quickly Felicity tried to piece together Mr. Haskall's reasoning. He'd have known his horses couldn't outrun Penny; that must be why he'd left them. Penny couldn't follow him through the woods, and Felicity, in her skirts, could never hope to catch him on foot. He must have expected that Felicity would give up chasing him and turn back. And even on foot he knew he would reach Yorktown and board his ship long before Felicity could get back to King's Creek and summon help. So his escape was assured. Or so he thought.

"He doesn't know about Father," Felicity murmured. By this time, she hoped, Father would be on his way from Williamsburg on this very path. Mr. Haskall would have to pass him in order to get to Yorktown.

But Father would be looking for someone riding Penny, not a man on foot. If Felicity didn't catch up with Mr. Haskall before he met Father, Father would let him go by and Mr. Haskall would go on to Yorktown and pass the maps to the British.

Felicity hated the idea of going after Mr. Haskall, now that it seemed clear that he would not change his mind. She hadn't a clue how she could stop him from carrying out his plans, but she knew she had to try. She could never live with herself if she gave up now and her beloved King's Creek Plantation ended up in flames. She swallowed hard and grasped a fistful of Penny's mane. The silky feel of it between her fingers somehow gave her resolve.

Her mind made up, she eased Penny over to Duchess and unfastened Duchess from Eclipse. Then, slapping the two riderless horses on the rump, she sent them off. Duchess would head straight home for breakfast, and Felicity hoped that Eclipse would follow.

"Now, Penny," she said, "let's go after Mr. Haskall."

Penny's ears pricked forward eagerly, and she responded immediately to the press of Felicity's heels against her side. She flung herself into a canter along the path, but Felicity reined her down to a brisk trot. She wanted to be able to survey the woods for Mr. Haskall as they passed. Mr. Haskall would have to come out of the woods eventually, she figured, to get back on the path, if he wanted to make it to Yorktown.

As Penny skimmed along, Felicity's eyes

probed the shadowy forest and the branches and leaves of brush, alert to any breath of movement that might mean Mr. Haskall was there. In spite of her determination, her heart was thudding in her chest nearly as loud as the thud of Penny's hooves on the path. She stared so hard into the wall of green that her eyes blurred, and she had to blink to clear them.

Soon the path wound up a steep hill, and Felicity felt the tautness of Penny's muscles as she strained forward for the climb. When they crested the hill, Felicity saw far up ahead some figures standing in the path, men with horses. Her heart leaped hopefully. Was Father among them?

As Felicity squinted to try to make them out, Penny threw up her head, jerking the reins from Felicity's hands, and galloped toward the men, nickering. Felicity, at first startled by Penny's misbehavior, realized in an instant why she had done it.

It *was* Father! Penny must have picked up

the scent of her stablemates in Williamsburg, Blossom and Father's mare, Old Bess. Now Felicity could see Father's long red hair, tied back in a queue, and the blue coat he always wore. With him were Marcus, the slave who helped Father in the store, and Mr. Wythe, one of their neighbors in Williamsburg.

And standing beside Father, talking to him, was Mr. Haskall!

Everything happened fast then, though it seemed to Felicity as if it happened in the plodding motion of a nightmare: Mr. Haskall turning to look at her, his jaw dropping open in shock, his eyes going wide; Penny's head bobbing and her shoulders stretching with each stride; Mr. Haskall's arms lifting and pumping as he broke into a run and dashed toward the woods; the shouts of Father and the men in reaction; Mr. Haskall vanishing into the concealing green of the trees.

Felicity pulled Penny to a halt in front of Father. "Father," she cried. "You must stop him! That's Mr. Haskall. He's the spy!"

"Felicity!" Father said, grabbing Penny's reins and helping Felicity slide from her back. "I'm confused. Ben said we should watch for a man riding Penny, but here you are on her instead. And now you say the man we were just talking to is your spy?"

"Yes!" Felicity said, her breath short. "You can't let him get away." As quickly as she could, she filled them in about Mr. Haskall's spying. "And I'm certain he has the maps with him, Father," she rushed on. "If he makes it to Yorktown, he'll turn the maps over to Lord Dunmore. And it will be too late to save the Patriot plantations!"

Father's face was grim. "Then there's no time to lose. Marcus and I'll go after him. Mr. Wythe, will you take my daughter back to the house?"

"Oh, Father, please let me wait here with Mr. Wythe," Felicity said. "I couldn't stand waiting at home, not knowing whether or not Mr. Haskall was caught."

"Very well," said Father. "Let's go, Marcus!"

Then Father and Marcus dashed into the woods after Mr. Haskall.

Felicity and Mr. Wythe sat down in the shade while the horses cropped grass at the edge of the path. Mr. Wythe tried to make conversation, but Felicity was too tense to talk much. She answered politely, but her mind was on Father and Marcus. It seemed they had been gone forever.

At last she heard the crash of foliage, and the men appeared out of the woods. Mr. Haskall was walking in front of Father, his hands tied in front of him. His hair had come loose and was hanging disheveled on his shoulders, snarled with twigs and leaves. His stockings were torn and his breeches were dirty. Marcus was carrying the haversack.

Felicity and Mr. Wythe stood up as Father and Marcus approached with Mr. Haskall. Father prodded Mr. Haskall forward, in front of Felicity. Mr. Haskall stood stiffly, his face closed. Felicity's gaze dropped to his shoes.

She saw that his silver shoe buckles were covered with mud.

Her mind flashed back to the day that she and Ben had come upon him beside the creek. That was the day she had first become suspicious of Mr. Haskall, and it was his shiny shoe buckles that had made her think he was lying. An ache rose in her chest for the loss of the friend she had thought he was.

"Felicity, is this the man you believe to be a spy?" Father asked.

A lump in Felicity's throat kept her from answering. It was so strange to be facing Mr. Haskall this way. She thought of all the time they had spent together, all the talks they had had. How could he have betrayed her? Maybe there was another explanation for everything that had happened. Surely he would tell her now if she gave him the chance.

"Mr. Haskall," she said fiercely. "You took Duchess—and Mr. Peabody's mare Midnight, too."

For a moment his eyes locked with Felicity's. Then he looked away. He didn't deny it. The lump in her throat got bigger. There *had* to be an explanation! She tried once more. "The maps you made," she said. "What were they for?"

His eyebrows went up. "Maps, Miss Merriman?" His tone was puzzled. "Whatever do you mean?"

Felicity drew her breath in sharply. What was it Mr. Haskall had said about carrying out secret plans? *At the very least you might intentionally mislead someone.* He was doing that now, she knew—trying to mislead her. Her heart sank.

Mr. Haskall stepped toward Felicity, smiling warmly. She didn't smile back.

"Father," she said softly, "if you search him, you'll find maps of the Patriot plantations along the York." She could feel Mr. Haskall looking at her, but she kept her eyes on the ground.

It seemed an eternity before Father replied.

Finally, he said to Mr. Haskall, "Sir, if you would consent to a search..."

"As you wish," said Mr. Haskall, lifting his arms, hands still bound, straight out from his body. "You may search me, but you'll find no maps."

Father ran his hands up and down Mr. Haskall's body, patting as he went. He loosed Mr. Haskall's hands and made him remove his coat and waistcoat and turn out the contents of his pockets: a timepiece and a change purse, but no maps. While Father searched Mr. Haskall, Mr. Wythe went through the haversack, where he found a folder of papers. Felicity waited tensely as Mr. Wythe shuffled through the papers. "No maps here," he finally said. "Nothing but drawings and notes about plants, it seems."

"As I told you, sir," said Mr. Haskall, holding his hands outstretched, palms outward, "no maps."

For a second, Felicity stood frozen with disbelief. She had been so sure Mr. Haskall would have the maps with him, to turn them over to whomever he was meeting in York-town. Had he lost the maps during the chase, or hidden them in the woods somewhere? Her thoughts ran feverishly, until her eyes landed on Mr. Haskall's shoe buckles, and an idea burst into her mind.

"Look in his shoes, Father!" she exclaimed.

Mr. Haskall's face turned white. He jumped forward as if to run, but Father caught hold of him. "Will you remove your shoes, sir? Or shall I do it for you?" Father demanded.

Mr. Haskall's eyes flicked toward Felicity for just an instant, but she couldn't read what was in them. Then he bent to remove his shoes and handed them to Father.

Astonishment showed on Father's face as he pulled out of Mr. Haskall's shoe a thick fold of foolscap. Felicity knew without being told that these were the maps. A weight seemed to slip from her shoulders, even while pain twisted inside her at this undeniable proof that Mr. Haskall had betrayed her.

Father's mouth was clamped shut as
he unfolded the foolscap and examined it.
Felicity waited tensely for Father to speak,
to say aloud what she already knew: that
on the foolscap were drawn maps of every
Patriot plantation in the area, including their
own. Finally she could stay quiet no longer.
She had to hear it from Father's own mouth.
"Are they the maps?" she asked.

The creases around Father's eyes had
deepened into hard lines. He didn't answer
Felicity. Instead, he said to Mr. Haskall,
"I trust that you will have an explanation
for carrying and concealing these maps
when you appear before the magistrate in
Williamsburg."

Felicity looked toward Mr. Haskall, but
his head was lowered, his shoulders hunched,
like a turtle in its shell. Suddenly, she felt
furious with him. "You *are* a spy!" she burst
out. "How could you!"

He looked up, his expression sorrowful.
"Miss Merriman, you must understand. My

first loyalty is to my king." His eyes searched her face, as if begging her for something. She shook her head, not knowing what he wanted and too angry to care.

Then she realized there *was* something, at the edge of her mind, that she thought she should remember. At first she couldn't pull it out, and then it came to her: his words about loyalty, the day she had shown him the path to Yorktown.

*Loyalty is complex,* he had said. *Sometimes a person may feel loyalty to two people or ideals that are opposed to one another . . . a decision must be made about which of the two should come first, and often there is regret that one must be forsaken for the other . . .*

They had been talking about Felicity's helping Penny escape from Jiggy Nye. Or at least Felicity had *thought* that was what they were talking about. Had Mr. Haskall been preparing her, even then, for the time when she would know that he had betrayed her trust?

For a split second she felt sympathy for

him, but she pushed it away. He had been willing to bring about the ruin of King's Creek Plantation! And the plantations of all their friends and neighbors!

She met Mr. Haskall's gaze, but she said nothing in reply. To her thinking, he had given up the privilege of a friend's understanding when he headed to Yorktown with the maps.

Father told Marcus to refasten Mr. Haskall's hands. "And secure the knots well," Father added. "I have a feeling this gentleman may be inclined toward escape."

For some reason, Felicity couldn't bear to watch Marcus tie up Mr. Haskall. She turned her back to him and stroked Penny's glossy neck. When Marcus finished, he prodded Mr. Haskall toward Blossom, intending, Felicity guessed, to fasten the rope around Mr. Haskall's hands to Blossom's saddle.

As Mr. Haskall passed Felicity and Penny, Penny thrust out her nose and nuzzled his shoulder. "There now, Penny," said Mr. Haskall gently. "You be a good girl now."

A sob caught in Felicity's throat. There *had* been a bond of friendship between Penny and Mr. Haskall... and between Mr. Haskall and Felicity. And now it was broken. Felicity was afraid she was going to cry, and she didn't want to. Then Marcus led Mr. Haskall past them, to Blossom.

Felicity felt Father's hand on her shoulder. He motioned for her to come aside with him. They stepped off the road into the shade of a big pine tree, its branches sighing above them in a breeze.

"I want you to know, Lissie," Father said, "how proud I am of you. You acted decisively and bravely, and you very well may have saved King's Creek Plantation, as well as the property of our neighbors. You've aided the Patriot cause as much as any soldier."

Then he noticed Felicity's downcast face. Gently he tilted up her chin. "My daughter, why do you look so sad?"

"Oh, Father!" said Felicity, trying so hard to hold back a sob that her lips trembled.

"I know I did the right thing. But I feel so confused, and so miserable. Mr. Haskall was my friend. Yet look what he did!"

"This is a confounded time, Lissie," said Father. "We're at war with our mother country, and many adults are just as confused and unhappy as you are. There are good people on both sides of this war. Remember that your grandfather was loyal to the king."

"But Grandfather would never have betrayed the people he cared about, even for the king!"

"No, he wouldn't have," said Father quietly.

Felicity's face was thoughtful. "Father, what will happen to Mr. Haskall?"

"I can't answer that question, Lissie," Father said. "There will be a trial in Williamsburg, and his fate will depend upon the outcome."

"Will Mr. Haskall have a chance to tell his side of the story?" she asked.

"He will."

Felicity nodded. Mr. Haskall was a good talker. He had a way of explaining that made you understand him and agree with him. Perhaps things would go well for him at his trial; perhaps not. Felicity didn't want to think beyond that.

Then Father left Felicity under the tree and went to speak to Mr. Wythe. Felicity saw Mr. Wythe and Marcus mount their horses. Mr. Haskall was on foot behind Blossom. In a moment Father came back to Felicity. He was leading Old Bess and smiling.

"Well, now, Daughter," he said, "since you have made our plantation home safe from the British, shall we head along in that direction? The morning has scarce begun, yet you and Penny have completed a full day's work. I think a fine big breakfast is in order, don't you? Especially on such a beautiful morning as this."

"Oh, yes, Father!" Felicity cried.

It *was* a beautiful morning. Felicity had been too anxious about Mr. Haskall to notice it

before. Now, as she and Father rode back along
the bridle path toward King's Creek,
she delighted in the soft warmth of the sun,
the satiny summer smell of the woods, and
the sweet songs of the birds. The day stretched
before her, golden and full of promise, just as
the summer did. Felicity was eager to begin
them both.

# LOOKING BACK

# A PEEK INTO THE PAST

*British soldiers setting fire to Patriot crops*

During the summer of 1776, tensions ran high between Patriots and Loyalists in the American colonies. Patriots, like Felicity's family, wanted the colonies to be free from British rule and taxes. Loyalists, like the Wentworths, thought that the colonies should remain loyal to the king of England. Fighting had already begun between the British army and the Patriot army, led by George Washington.

Just the summer before, the British governor of Virginia had fled Williamsburg and moved onto a British ship in the harbor at Yorktown.

From there, Governor Dunmore fought the Patriots by ordering raids on their farms and plantations. Dunmore's troops burned houses, stables, and barns. They stole crops and livestock to feed British troops, or

*Governor Dunmore*

they destroyed the crops to prevent them from being used by the Patriots. And the raiders took some of the Patriots' finest horses to offer to British soldiers.

Sometimes the British sent out spies to find and map out the best places to make raids. Williamsburg was a target because it lay between the James and York rivers. British raiders could sail up those rivers, close to Williamsburg, without being spotted.

Other targets were plantations owned by Patriots attending the

*A British soldier mounted on a fine horse*

Virginia Convention in Williamsburg. Men from all over Virginia had gathered to vote on whether Virginia should support independence for the colonies. The delegates voted in favor of the Resolution for Independence. Just after voting, the men took down the British flag flying over the Capitol and replaced it with the Grand Union flag of Washington's army.

A representative from the Virginia Convention set off for Philadelphia to share Virginia's vote with the Continental Congress. There, a committee including John Adams, Benjamin Franklin, and Thomas Jefferson drew up a document declaring the colonies independent from England. Jefferson wrote the declaration in just two weeks during June of 1776, exactly when Felicity's mystery takes place.

Jefferson fought the British not with a weapon but with a quill pen. Many Americans also chose to fight without taking up arms. Women weren't allowed to fight as soldiers in the war, but they fought in

*Patriot Catherine Schuyler fought back with fire.*

other ways. Catherine Schuyler feared that the British would steal her farm's wheat, which was ready for harvesting. Rather than allow the British to take the wheat, Catherine took a torch and set fire to her own fields.

Other women risked their lives by serving as spies for the Patriot army. They made perfect spies because no one thought that they could understand military matters. Women proved them wrong by volunteering to carry messages for the Patriot army or to gather information by listening in on British military conversations.

Girls got in on the action, too. Sixteen-year-old Sybil Ludington dreamed of helping the war effort by being a Patriot soldier. When her father learned that British troops had set fire to a nearby city, he needed someone to ride through the countryside to summon the Patriot soldiers. Sybil bravely volunteered.

Just as Felicity makes a daring ride on horseback to protect her neighbors, Sybil rode Star, her family's stallion, from farm to farm. Sybil rode more than 40 miles in three hours and summoned more than 400 soldiers to fight. The soldiers drove the British back to their ships. General George Washington himself visited Sybil to thank her for her courage. Her brave ride on horseback had made her a hero. When the Declaration of Independence was approved on

*A statue of Sybil Ludington in Carmel, New York, honors her daring ride.*

*The signing of the Declaration of Independence*

July 4, 1776, the Patriots still had five long years of fighting ahead of them. But the declaration restored their spirits and their hunger for independence.

Fighting from the home front gave women a new sense of independence, too, and changed their beliefs about what they could and couldn't do. These women and their daughters laid the foundation for another revolution that would come years later—the fight for equal rights for women.

# ABOUT THE AUTHOR

 Elizabeth McDavid Jones has lived most of her life in North Carolina, usually near woods and creeks. Her earliest passions were animals and writing. As a girl, she especially loved to write stories about animals.

Today, she lives in Virginia with her husband and children. She is the author of three mysteries about Felicity Merriman: *Peril at King's Creek, Traitor in Williamsburg,* and *Lady Margaret's Ghost.*

She also wrote five American Girl History Mysteries: *The Night Flyers,* which won the Edgar Allan Poe Award for Best Children's Mystery; *Secrets on 26th Street; Watcher in the Piney Woods; Mystery on Skull Island;* and *Ghost Light on Graveyard Shoal,* an Agatha Award nominee for Best Children's/Young Adult Mystery.

Enjoy all of these American Girl Mysteries®:

*and many more!*